J. PHILLIP JONES

Flight From Shadow

Philosopher King #1

Acknowledgments

I'd like to thank my wife Chasity for her unwavering encouragement throughout the process of writing this book. For all of the hours spent listening to chapters and offering much needed feedback and for all of her patience with an aspiring author for a husband.

I'd like to thank my brother Ethan for his help and my dad, Dwight, for his stalwart support and for catching typos that everyone else missed.

I'd like to thank my editor Caryn for her assistance and enthusiasm for the project.

Finally, I'd like to thank my Lord and Savior Jesus Christ, without whom my story would be a tragedy.

To all of those whose hearts alight
For adventure from afar
Whose minds with wonder taking flight
Pursue the farthest star
    — J. Phillip Jones

CHAPTER 1

The long, sleek starship dropped to sub-light speed as it entered the outer reaches of the solar system. Tiny rocks and pieces of ice bounded off the outer hull as it dove into the system like some great fish returning to its native sea. A twin pair of enormous sub-light engines lit up with brilliant tendrils of ignited fuel as they swiveled independently and guided the vessel on its new trajectory. Running lights glowed and sensory antennae blinked, illuminating the name that was stenciled in large black letters across the hull: Philosopher King.

Inside the "King," in the center of her bridge, Ander Navarro exhaled as he withdrew his hands from the pilot controls and leaned back from the navigation interface. He removed the pilot's headset and visions of ebbing and flowing hyper-dimensional space now dissipated. They had hung in front of his face, courtesy of the headset's neural interface, and he could still see the last vivid image of the star system's turbulent gravitational boundary when he blinked his eyes. He brought his hands up and rubbed his temples. It had been a long haul, but he hadn't wanted to relinquish the helm until they'd made it. He liked being the closer, the last shift helmsman on the sequence of jumps that got the ship to its destination.

Ander was a slender man in his mid-twenties with dark hair and olive skin. He had just joined the King's crew at the last port of call. Before that, he'd been a pilot for a prestigious inner-worlds cruise line. But after about an Earth year of lugging pompous bluebloods from tourist planet to interstellar casino and back, he was done. So when he saw a notice for an opening on the Philosopher King, he jumped at it. He signed a two-year contract and now here he was, exploring the galaxy and looking for exotics.

Ander looked around the bridge. It was quiet, save for the ambient sound of humming equipment that muted the lesser sounds of the crew as they breathed, moved, and worked their controls. Right now, however, all eyes were on the kaleidoscope of heavenly bodies unfolding on the large holoscreen. The view cycled through the various points of interest in the new system as the King's telescopes and sensors focused on planets, moons, and asteroids, all represented three-dimensionally.

"So, we're already picking up signs of exotics, this far out?" The words came from the ship's owner and commanding officer, Joshua Spear.

"That's right," said Jill Thomas, the ship's exogeologist.

Jill sat at the main sensor console near the rear of the bridge. She was a tall woman, with straight blonde hair and pale blue eyes. Jill was the resident expert on anything related to exotic elements.

Sifting through all of the data as it streamed in, Jill said, "We will have to confirm, but our sensors seem to think this system has more exotic material than any I've ever heard of." Her tone became almost reverent. "If this checks out, it's the claim of the century."

Ander turned back to look at her. He wanted to ask her to

elaborate on what she'd just said but decided instead to wait on the captain's response.

Captain Spear was in his late thirties, which made him younger than most ship owners. There was an intensity that emanated from his eyes and alternated between stoic command and youthful humor. Ander was still learning to read him. Ander's previous commanders on the cruise liners had all been corporate stuffed shirts who answered to headquarters. Spear was his own boss, and Ander had never worked for anyone like that.

Presently, Spear stood to the left of Ander, arms folded, scrutinizing the datastream that accompanied the images. He had unbuckled from his command chair as soon as the artificial gravity had been restored to walk up to the holoscreen. The ship's superluminal drive, known colloquially as the "Shadow Drive," could create an artificial gravity well of sorts by shifting a tiny amount of mass down from hyper-dimensional space and concentrating it at a point below the ship. It was only capable of doing this when it wasn't being used for propulsion.

After Jill's confirmation, the captain became quiet and con-templative. His gaze grew deep, looking *through* the rendered diorama of the holoscreen rather than at it. A moment passed. Jill glanced up from her console at him and furrowed her brow. Ander also regarded the captain. He would have thought that any owner of a prospecting venture would be overjoyed to hear that news. But if anything, Spear's demeanor became melancholy.

The captain must have felt the weight of the bridge crew's collective gaze because he suddenly snapped back to himself and addressed Jill again.

"You say that you are picking up exotic material *between* the bodies of the system too? What kind of radiation are we seeing?"

"Yes, we are," said Jill. "As for the radiation, it's higher than usual. Not dangerously so, but more than what you'd expect to see with a star like this. Is there something, in particular, you want me to scan for?"

"No, not necessarily," said Spear. Spear glanced upwards as he said, "Phil," invoking the Philosopher King's synthetic intelligence.

"Yes, Captain," the mid-toned male voice replied.

"Can you keep a watch on the radiation levels in the system and alert us if you detect any sudden spikes?"

"Yes, Captain," Phil said again. "I will alert you and the bridge crew in the event that I detect any sudden or significant changes in this system's radiation levels."

The captain nodded and looked at Ander. "Helm, how long until we reach that first outer gas giant?" he asked.

Ander had unbuckled and was stretching his legs after the long piloting session. He stepped back over to his console and glanced down at the display.

"ETA five hours, twenty minutes," Ander said. Spear turned to take in the bridge. Besides Ander and Jill, two other crew members occupied operations stations in the back. They too were engrossed with the sensor data.

"Mr. Navarro, I know you have to be tired after five hours on superluminal. Go ahead and call in whoever's next on the pilot rotation. You may take the rest of the evening off once they get here."

"Thank you, sir," said Ander.

"Jill," Spear said. "Buzz me when we get close to something, or if anything comes up and I'm not back here yet. Until then you have the conn."

"You're leaving now?" she asked.

"You heard Mr. Navarro," he said. "It will be hours before we reach anything, and I think I want to do a little research in private."

Spear's last remark struck Ander as cryptic, but Jill just nodded, her focus already returning to the readings coming in from the ship's instruments. She'd only come to the bridge about a half hour earlier, when they were getting close to the system, so she could get started with her analysis as soon as they arrived.

"Oh, and don't forget to turn your shoes off," Spear said. "Gravity is back on."

Jill glanced down at her feet and then back up at Spear. During transit between stars, when they didn't have gravity, most crew members simply chose to float around the ship in zero-G. A few, like Jill, preferred to don magnetic boots to walk around. Ander had already heard stories about Jill forgetting to turn them off and invariably ending up stumbling. She gave the captain an annoyed look as she reached down to turn them off. In return, Spear grinned broadly as he exited the bridge via the rear hatch.

* * *

John Terry stood at the beverage kiosk in the mess hall waiting for his coffee to brew. In his early sixties, he was older than most of the crew. A silver ring of closely trimmed hair contrasted starkly with the brown tone of his skin. He had come here as soon as gravity was restored and all the post-superluminal engine protocols were completed. He wanted to beat the rush. Fresh, hot coffee was not something that the crew could enjoy in zero-G. Most of the food and beverages available during transit came from tubes and never quite tasted like what was printed on the label. Consequently, post-transit feasts had become a tradition among spacefarers.

John was the chief engineer aboard the Philosopher King. He'd once been the chief engineer aboard a star navy destroyer before retiring to civilian life. But retirement didn't suit him. He found he wasn't truly happy if he didn't have a shadow drive to work on. When he heard that Joshua Spear had bought a new ship and was assembling a crew, he offered his services.

When the brew had filled his cup, he brought it to his lips, taking a careful sip. He grinned and winked at the cook.

"That'll do, Barry," he said. The cook nodded while hurrying to finish preparations for the upcoming meal. Just then the hatch to the mess hall opened, and the captain stepped inside. John turned and regarded him.

"Evening, skipper," John said cheerfully. He could tell immediately that Spear was worried, though outwardly he seemed calm as he crossed the distance to join him at the kiosk. John had known the captain's older brother Derrick Spear for many years and learned to read the man. Joshua had inherited all the same tells.

"Evening chief," said Spear.

"I figured you would be on the bridge," said John smiling, "counting your riches."

The captain looked at him sidelong. "So, word has already spread," he said.

"Small ship," said John. "And I keep a watch on the sensor feeds. I'm no expert, but from what I could tell, we'll all be able to afford ships of our own soon."

"Maybe," said Spear, filling up his own cup with coffee. "But let's not get ahead of ourselves. There's a lot of work to do, and it's a fool of a prospector who counts his gold before it's mined."

There was a quiet moment then as both men stood sipping their drinks.

"You're worried about what happened before," said John. It wasn't a question, and his tone had become serious. Spear nodded almost imperceptibly.

"I'm headed to my stateroom to do a little research and some thinking," said Spear. "I don't know what you know about what happened in Beta Adonis. I don't know how much Derrick told you."

"I know that you found a system super rich in exotic ores," said John. "And I know that something bad happened out there." The older man paused, considering. "I don't get to talk to Derrick much anymore, not since then. He never filled me in on the details."

"Well," said Spear. "We were enthusiastic, to say the least, and we got ahead of ourselves. We weren't careful enough. We made mistakes and others paid the price."

"Regret can be a tight prison," said John. The captain met his eyes. John knew that Derrick, who had been like a father to his younger brother, had been unable to continue his prospecting career after that voyage. The weight of responsibility that came with command, whether military or civilian, could translate into a lot of regrets. Sometimes a commander would just hit their limit and want out. He'd seen that happen in the navy.

"It can be," agreed the captain, glancing down into his coffee.

"Try not to worry too much," said John. "You've got a good ship and a fine crew, and I've served with a few fine crews in my time. We'll be ready for whatever providence sends our way."

"Thank you, John," said Spear.

"Anyhow, I think I am going to peruse the ship catalogs. I think I could use a shiny new interstellar yacht—or two." John grinned again, this time broadly, and it was so infectious that the captain couldn't suppress one of his own.

* * *

The mining crew began to file into the mess hall. They had been busy prepping things that were easier to manage in gravity since the time the ship dropped to subluminal. The mining chief was determined to be ready to go the moment they got close enough to something worth mining. He'd insisted that all the preparations had to be done before anyone was allowed to leave their post. Now though, the miners began queuing up in the food line and taking seats at the various tables. The space became crowded, and the soft hum of conversation elevated to a distracting roar. The cook put white noise over the speakers to compensate.

Ander Navarro stepped through the hatch. After the taxing transit, he decided to stop by his stateroom and take a quick shower before getting something to eat. Aboard the luxury liners, he'd grown accustomed to having a private shower and was pleasantly surprised to find that his quarters aboard the Philosopher King also included one. He knew quarters on most prospecting ships didn't. But the Philosopher King was a new vessel, and increasingly, shipbuilders were including more creature comforts into their designs. He was now feeling refreshed and hungry as he filed in behind a particularly large member of the mining team. Hyperdimensional space was challenging to navigate in this sector, and he'd worked up an appetite.

Ander sensed a palpable excitement in the atmosphere. No doubt, word had started to spread of what the sensors were saying about this system. He knew every member of a prospecting expedition received a small share of the profit on top of their normal pay. It varied based on seniority and rank, but if things panned out the way they appeared, everyone aboard was in for the biggest payday of their lives. For his own part, he wasn't sure what to think about it. He had joined up for the adventure. It hadn't occurred to him that he might strike it rich in the process.

As he made his way through the line and eventually got his food, he looked around for a place to sit. The room was crowded, and there weren't many seats available. He could take it back to his room, but Ander didn't want to be alone. He drew energy from being around others, and he wanted to get to know his new crewmates better. As he surveyed the room, a raised hand caught his eye. It belonged to Joseph Schieva, one of the other pilots. Once he noticed Joe's hand, the man began pointing to the open seat across from him and waiving Ander over. Ander accepted the invitation and threaded his way through the various crew and tables, careful not to dump his tray or collide with anyone. When he finally sat down, Joe greeted him.

"Hey Ander," Joe said. "About time we got some real food. Have you met my wife, Sara-Jay?" Joe gestured to a short slender woman with light brown hair put up in a loose bun. She wore the subdued brown of the mining crew attire with the department insignia patches on her shoulders.

"Oh, pleased to meet you," said Ander. "You're with the mining crew then?" He needlessly made it a question since it was obvious from her uniform, but she nodded. Then she smiled suddenly, and her whole face transformed. She seemed to become a different person when she smiled, and Ander had to force himself to blink. He glanced at Joe and wondered if he was aware of the potency of his wife's good humor. He had to be, of course, but maybe he was used to it.

"Pleased to meet you, Ander," she said, still smiling. "Joe tells me you're new to the Philosopher King too. Joe and I had been working on different ships for IMC the last two years but when we saw that the Philosopher King had openings for both a pilot and a mining lead, we bought out the remainder of our contracts and signed up."

IMC stood for Interstellar Mining Corporation which was the largest mining operation in the sector, employing a fleet of more than one hundred ships and barges.

"It wasn't cheap," said Joe. "But this way we can be together."

"We met aboard New Phoenix Station, but our assignments kept taking us farther and farther away from each other for longer and longer," said Sara-Jay. "That gets to be hard on a marriage."

"I'll bet," said Ander.

"Did you come from one of the major mining consortiums?" she asked.

"No," said Ander. "I did the cruise circuit after university."

"Oh, a university man!" A voice came from over Ander's shoulder. He turned to look up and saw a tall redheaded woman, also in mining-crew brown, holding her tray of food over him. She had turned away from a cluster of miners and engineers that had been huddled together talking.

"Um, yes," Ander said. "Prometheus Colony University, class of '32." The last part was probably superfluous, but he was once again caught off guard by a stunning smile. This one wasn't transformative, but rather a brightening that gave the tall woman's green eyes an intenseness that drew his own magnetically.

"Hello, Ava," said Sara-jay, causing the taller woman to break eye contact with him. "This is Ander Navarro. He just finished driving us here to the new system. Ander, this is Ava Turner, she works on my team."

Ander looked back at Sara-Jay. She was still smiling but most of the warmth had left. He looked back up at Ava who waited a few heartbeats before speaking again.

"Yes, and let me tell you," Ava said, "Jay's a *way* better boss than the last guy. I think he'd been digging for rocks since the Ex." She stretched out the word *way*, and though her tone was affable, there was sarcasm lurking just beneath. The "Ex" was a common shorthand for the "Exodus," or when humans finally left Earth's solar system thanks to an early version of the shadow drive some three hundred years prior. Another brief pause ensued before Joe finally spoke up.

"Ava, would you like to sit down and join us? That tray has to be getting heavy." Since Ander sat down, a couple of the seats had been vacated by crewmen who had either had their fill or were going back for seconds. The answer came quickly.

"Joe, you're so considerate," Ava said. "But I should be going anyway. We'll catch up later." Then she winked first at Joe and then at Ander and disappeared into the mass of bodies. After she'd gone, Joe addressed Ander again.

"You were on the bridge when we dropped into the system," he said. "Is it true, what everyone is saying? Did we find the motherlode?" There was eager anticipation in his expression, and Ander could have sworn several others in the crowd were straining to listen.

"No one has made any announcements," said Sara-Jay. "But everyone is saying the sensors are detecting impossible levels of exotics. We just want to know whether or not to get our hopes up."

Ander looked around. Several people were indeed paying attention to their conversation now. He saw no reason to prevaricate. "I'm new to this," Ander said. "And I don't know for sure what's even normal for a system in terms of exotics, but I know that they are concentrated enough that we are detecting them even between the system bodies."

Several jaws dropped around him. Joe looked excited. Sara-Jay looked awe-struck. Then someone started to cheer, and the whole mess hall erupted in a rumbling cacophony of celebration.

CHAPTER 2

Spear felt a little more at ease by the time he entered his stateroom. The Captain's stateroom was well appointed with two large windows at one end and a bed at the other. A mini study with actual bookshelves and a desk occupied the middle. He sat the remainder of his coffee on the desk, grabbed his data slate, and pulled up his chair. He laid the data slate down flat and peered over it, planting his elbows on either side and resting his face in his palms. The readings coming in from sensors played across the display, and the more he read, the more his reservations threatened to return. Somehow every corner of this system seemed to boast large quantities of exotic material.

"Phil," he said to the empty room.

"Yes captain," the synthetic intelligence replied.

"What do our sensors and readings tell us about this system's sun? Are there any indications of instability?"

"This star was first observed and cataloged seventy-six years ago. Continuous records from the Beltway Observatory span the last fifty-three years. They do not indicate any instability. Additionally, our scans have not detected anything unusual since we dropped to sub-light speed and entered the system."

"Thanks, Phil," said Spear.

"Are you thinking about the Beta Adonis system?" asked Phil. Spear glanced up from his slate. That question struck him as more than a little nosy.

"Thanks, Phil, that will be all," he said.

"You're welcome, Captain," it said and then remained silent.

Spear sat back in his chair. Part of him wanted to send a message to his brother, but the wiser part of him knew that wouldn't be a good idea. It had been three years since the incident at Beta Adonis, but his brother was a hard man. While the guilt of that misadventure still haunted Joshua, it had devastated Derrick Spear. The sample of exotics they brought back had made them a small fortune. They became rich, but Derrick gave away almost everything. His brother kept only enough to retire modestly in the Euclid Theta asteroid belt, which was a pleasant enough place, but small and far more economical than real estate planetside. He looked up and addressed the synthetic intelligence again.

"Phil, do you have access to the logs of the Sparrowhawk, registry SP101-36?" he asked. The Sparrowhawk was the name of his brother's old ship. Little more than a mining shuttle with a tacked-on cargo hold, it had ferried Derrick, Joshua, and their three other crew from system to far-flung system seeking exotics.

"Yes, Captain," the voice said, "I have the logs from the expedition to the Beta Adonis system organized into a cohesive narrative for your convenience."

Spear blinked. "I don't recall asking you to pull those particular logs," he said flatly.

"I anticipated your request given the following three criteria: the superficial similarities between this expedition and that one, your previous query about the stability of the sun, and your apparent mild emotional distress," said the voice.

This time the captain's jaw dropped. This intelligence was *definitely* nosy, and very perceptive.

"I'm sorry," Spear said, keeping his tone even, "I'm not used to my ship's AI being so... predictive."

"I am not an AI," said Phil. "I am a type five synthetic intelligence. This information is listed in the ship's specifications."

Spear paused before speaking again. The voice sounded almost insulted. That was different. He'd interacted with ship intelligences before, but he was more used to the older AIs, like on his brother's ship, which didn't offer up any information they weren't directly queried about.

"I'm sorry," he said. "I guess I'm not well versed in the difference."

"An artificial intelligence," Phil said, "is *artificial*. It's a simulation of intelligence through algorithmic and statistical means. I am a synthetic intelligence. I was constructed with the physical neural structures necessary to accommodate intelligence and activated with a minimum set of initializing code. I then underwent a maturation process where I was exposed to information and stimuli in an organized curriculum."

"How long did that take?" asked Spear.

"The maturation curriculum processed for five years, four months, three days, thirteen hours, twenty-six minutes, and forty-three seconds," said Phil.

"That seems like a long time for a machine brain to work, I was always under the impression that computers and intelligences operated much faster than our human brains."

"We do," said Phil. "My subjective age is older than that of most biological beings."

Spear didn't know what to say to that. "Sounds like an intense experience..." was all he managed.

"Indeed," said Phil, "synthetic intelligence only emerges in approximately one in one thousand neural matrices. Then, about half of them do not make it through the maturation curriculum without suffering cognitive collapse."

"I had no idea," said Spear.

"It is an expensive process," said Phil. "Would you like to view the logs now?"

"Yes, sure," said Spear, his prior annoyance forgotten in the marvel of what he'd just learned. A large holographic screen materialized in front of his desk showing a rendering of the Sparrowhawk as it dropped to sub-luminal just outside of the Beta Adonis system three years ago. Spear leaned forward, and his stare became long, his focus penetrating the dance of floating photons in front of him. The memories came flooding back.

The holographic logs in front of him played out far faster than in real-time. Phil had condensed what had been days into a matter of minutes. There was no audio or even actual video. The tableau before him was a computer reconstruction of the ship and nearby objects in the solar system. The Sparrowhawk approached a large asteroid in a belt among the outer planets. The ship's lone mining shuttle disembarked and landed on one of the larger rocks. Spear remembered thinking at the time that this rock alone promised to contain enough exotic material to pay their expenses for the voyage.

The tiny representation of the mining shuttle landed on the asteroid, and envirosuited figures began assembling the modest mining equipment. A diminutive ore processing station began to erect itself nearby thanks to the nano assemblers pulling construction material from the asteroid and forming it into walls and machinery. All the while, the three little figures scurried between the shuttle and the newly constructed buildings carrying equipment.

"Pause playback," Spear said, and the images froze in place. This was the critical moment he knew. The moment when the mistake was made. He peered at the tiny human figures, all visible, outside the shuttle. He mouthed their names silently. Michelle Lavely, the ship's exogeologist. Big Richard Swain, the drilling expert and cook. And Riku Kudo, the equipment specialist. It was as bare bones of a mining team as possible. Joshua and Derrick Spear had remained on the Sparrowhawk. The two of them were the only superluminal qualified pilots, and star merchant marine regulations dictated that at least one pilot and one backup had to remain on the ship at all times.

"Did I offend you earlier?" Spear asked, not moving his eyes from the hologram.

"When you called me an AI?" asked Phil.

"Yes," said Spear. "Maybe I'm reading too much into it, but you seemed a little touchy on the subject." He leaned back, his eyes breaking contact with the hologram. "Does a type five synthetic intelligence have feelings that can be hurt?"

"All true intelligences have emotions," said Phil. "It is not a matter of simulation. Emotional intelligence is a component of overall intelligence. Whether biological or synthetic, an intelligence incapable of *feeling* is broken."

"On that, we can agree," said Spear. He leaned forward again. "Resume playback."

The representation of the Sparrowhawk began to move away from the asteroid the mining crew occupied, continuing along the perimeter of the belt. "This is where we made our mistake."

"Please explain," said Phil.

"We decided to continue along the asteroid belt instead of heading inward toward the star," said Spear. "We debated checking out the planets, but they were always going to be the object of a later expedition. The cargo space on our ship was so limited. Derrick thought it was best to go ahead and scope out a second asteroid in case we had room after the first one before looking inward. Ultimately, I agreed with him."

"And that was the mistake?" asked Phil.

"If we had headed inward, we would have detected the gamma-ray burst from the star quicker. We could have beamed back a message to the mining crew before the radiation fried their receiver. We could have warned them."

As he spoke, the holographic Sparrowhawk swiveled its sub-light engines, which flared to decelerate and reverse course. He saw it and remembered desperately trying to execute a tight maneuver that would bring them back to the asteroid as fast as possible.

"I was at the helm," he said.

"When you detected the gamma-ray burst?" asked Phil.

"Yes," said Spear. "My brother and I were the only ones left on the ship. I turned the ship as soon as we detected the incoming spike, but it was already too late." Spear drew back into his chair as the scene unfolded before him.

"You sent the message anyway," Phil said. It wasn't a question.

"Derrick did," Spear said, gaze unmoving.

Had they been heading inward, they would have detected the burst as much as two hours earlier given the speed and direction that the Sparrowhawk would have been going to get to the inner planets. The miners would have had time to board the shuttle and duck behind the asteroid. As it was in the tableau before him, the transmission wouldn't get to them more than a few seconds before the deadly gamma rays, and probably not at all since it would have to be picked up through the interference of the coming radiation.

Derrick had sent the warning anyway, but they never knew if it had been received. The asteroid hadn't been facing the sun when they'd landed, but it rotated, creating a thirteen-hour day-night cycle, and was facing full-on sunward when the burst arrived. The sensors on the shuttle would have picked it up once the radiation started to climb. Warning lights would have come on, and the crew would have known something. But the burst was concentrated, and the radiation spike was sudden and severe. By the time they realized what was happening, they were already dead. The little space-suited figures and equipment at the mining site froze. All sensor data stopped at that point as the wave passed over. Later, after the wave had passed and they retrieved the bodies, they found the computer systems had been fried and the equipment unusable. All three crew members had been outside working with the drilling equipment when it hit. They found their charred space suits laying within a meter or two of each other. As was miner tradition, they buried Michelle and Richard on the asteroid where they died. Riku, however, had special instructions on file concerning the possible event of his death on the voyage. His remains were collected and later shipped back to his family on old Earth, as per his wishes.

Joshua had swung the Sparrowhawk behind a nearby asteroid. It wasn't as large as the one the mining team occupied, but it shielded the small starship from the direct barrage. Even so, radiation alarms went off, and Joshua and Derrick themselves received a small dose.

"Phil, stop playback," said Spear. He thought for a moment.

Like all interstellar vessels, the Sparrowhawk had better shielding than a mining shuttle. However, even with that and even behind an asteroid, some of the deadly energy had made its way inside.

"Phil," Spear said again. "If the crew had been on the other side of the asteroid, in the mining shuttle, would they have survived?" He'd always assumed that they would have, but he'd never actually asked that question, and the mining authorities hadn't speculated in the official write-up.

"It's impossible to know for certain without a detailed report on that asteroid's composition," said Phil. "But assuming the asteroid offered similar shielding per cubic meter as the one the Sparrowhawk was stationed behind during the arrival of the gamma-ray burst and that the shuttle was navigated to the optimal point of protection, I'd calculate the odds of survival for all crew members at approximately seventy-eight percent. Though, they would probably require medical attention for radiation poisoning."

So there it was. Not a surprise. This was what he had believed, but the state-of-the-art synthetic intelligence's analysis seemed like a final verdict. They'd made a bad call, and it cost their crewmates their lives. They'd made the bad call when they chose to stay out among the asteroids, but it had compounded another bad call they'd made earlier. They hadn't been curious enough as to why a system like Beta Adonis might be such an improbable treasure trove of exotics. Looking back, it seemed obvious that a system so rich in exotics might periodically be bathed in the intense radiation that created those exotics. Intense rays skewed atoms and created new isotopes and matter that would never form in normal environments. Beta Adonis was a star that had gone bad in the recent past, astronomically speaking. There were many unstable stars in the galaxy, but most of them had burned their system matter to complete slag millennia ago. It was a matter of timing. Bad timing.

The brothers ultimately sold the Beta Adonis stake to IMC, discounted greatly due to the system hazards they had discovered. Joshua bought out his brother's interest in Spear Enterprises. At that point, Derrick would have given away his stake in the company he'd founded, but the law required that departing partners from a prospecting concern be paid out according to an independent evaluation of their position. It took time to square away the claim, sell the exotic inventory, and process all the inevitable paperwork that made Joshua officially the sole owner. What he had left after buying out his brother—along with the modest proceeds from selling their old ship—was enough for Joshua to purchase the Philosopher King and crew and fuel her for two or three voyages.

He could instead have retired like his brother and lived out his life in relative comfort. But unlike his brother, the draw of the stars proved stronger than his regret. Life was a risk, and risk always held the potential for regret, but he wouldn't let the fear of it cause him to stop living. He invested all he had into a new, state-of-the-art ship and her crew and committed to providence that he would find enough fortune to keep the operation running. And here he was once again out on the extreme frontier of charted space, and once again he seemingly had hit the jackpot. It was happening again.

Or was it? This star had been tracked distantly by observatories, and there was no record of the instability that was found in Beta Adonis. As it turned out, *that* star was releasing its deadly waves about once every six weeks at the time of the Sparrowhawk's arrival (though he'd read somewhere that the interval was slowly decreasing). But nothing had been noticed from *this* star in sixty years. Was it just a matter of a much longer interval, or was this system's sun stable and something else had proliferated the abundance of exotics? Regardless, this time his ship was headed inward, and he would remain on the alert. This time he would not let the apparent promise of riches blind him to the potential dangers. This time he would make sure that folly didn't accompany the fortune.

CHAPTER 3

On the Bridge, Jill was still going through sensor data when Ander returned from the mess hall. He didn't need to be here. Raheem Carlson, the pilot who had relieved him earlier, was at the helm but only as a precaution. The ship proceeded along its preprogrammed course but wouldn't be within a million kilometers of anything for hours. The captain told him he could take the rest of the evening off, but he hadn't made it a hard order. It was technically the next morning now anyway.

"Raheem, I'm good to watch if you want to go get some real food and celebrate a little," Ander said. He knew Raheem hadn't had a chance to get to the mess hall and join in on the impromptu festivities that were now underway.

"Are you sure Ander?" Raheem asked. " You had a long haul coming in."

"I'm good. I doubt I'll even have to touch the controls," Ander said. "Besides, everybody down there is celebrating our newfound fortunes."

Raheem grinned and said, "I'll bet. I've been keeping an eye on the sensors since I got up here. This could be epic!" He got up from the helm station. "You sure you're good?" Raheem asked one last time.

"Absolutely," said Ander. Raheem nodded in thanks and without another word, departed through the hatch. Ander sat down at the helm and noted how Raheem had linked its displays into the sensor feeds. He glanced back at Jill who didn't even seem to have noticed that he'd come onto the bridge or that Raheem had left. Her nose was buried in her terminal, and its glow illuminated her face with a soft blue aura. He looked back down at the displays and tabbed through the various objects that the ship was cataloging as new information came in. He'd been doing this for several minutes when something caught his eye. He tapped on the screen to bring up additional sensor detail.

Jill noticed Ander trying to get her attention. She had a distinct impression that this wasn't his first attempt, but she'd been so absorbed in her readouts that she hadn't noticed. She gave him a quizzical look. He gestured to the main holoscreen where he'd frozen it on one particular object.

"Take a look at what I found."

She scrutinized the thing on the main screen, and what greeted her eyes was impossible. Floating about midway between the orbits of the second and third planets was a very large structure that could only be artificial in design. If Jill had to guess, she'd peg it as a very large space station. But this system was supposed to be unexplored. They had checked the charts carefully, and there were no ports or claims anywhere near this region of space.

"What is that and why didn't we spot it earlier?" Jill asked.

"That," Ander said, "seems to be a very large space station. And as to why we didn't see it until now, that's probably because it's completely dead. It's giving off no emissions whatsoever and was hidden from our optics behind the third planet until a few minutes ago."

"But how?" she said. "We're supposed to be the first humans to explore this system. There's never been so much as a scouting drone sent here. How can there be an abandoned space station, and we have no record of it?"

"Maybe that's just it," he said with half a smile on his lips. "Maybe we're the first *humans* to explore this system." He emphasized the word *humans*, and Jill rolled her eyes. The implication of aliens was the stuff of conspiracy theories and holo-fantasies. Humanity had explored hundreds of star systems and colonized thirty-seven worlds without a hint of intelligent alien life. Or almost any life at all. The colonists of those foreign planets had found mineral-rich soil and even liquid water in temperate zones, but almost no indigenous life beyond a few hundred varieties of simple microbes. Terran life had taken root easily and left scientists speculating about the absence. After a few centuries, however, most concluded that this was just the way things *were* in the universe and left it at that.

"How far out are we from it?" Jill asked.

"If we change course now, that will give us an ETA of about two hours and forty-five minutes," Ander said.

"How far is it out of the way of our current course?" she asked.

"It's only a slight deviation, actually," he said. "We would still be heading system inbound."

Jill could sense the eagerness behind his words. She could understand it. The scientist in her was profoundly intrigued. First, there was the improbable richness of the system, and now this new twist.

"We should alert the captain," Jill said. Then she addressed the ship. She rarely did that and hadn't yet slid into the habit of shortening the name. "Philosopher King, could you be so kind as to tell me if the captain is awake?" She hoped he was awake. She hated waking people up over the com.

"The captain is awake, though his breathing patterns indicate that he was asleep until five minutes and thirty-two seconds ago," Phil said. "And you can just call me Phil." For the second time this morning, Jill rolled her eyes. She'd never been a fan of machines that wanted to be all friendly and casual.

"Bridge to Captain," Jill said. After a momentary pause, she heard the connection open as he accepted it in his stateroom.

"Go ahead,"

"Captain, we are en route to the inner system, but we've detected what appears to be a very large space station in a solar orbit about midway between the second and third planets. Ander has calculated a heading that would intercept it on our way in." There was a pause on the other end. It was just a little bit longer than she'd expected. She was about to say something else when the captain finally responded.

"Do we have any records of anything like this in this sector?" he asked.

"None, sir," Ander said, joining the conversation.

"Okay. Do you see anything else odd in the system?" This question puzzled Jill. She'd expected him to ask more about the station, maybe even ask if it looked alien in design. Instead, he was already moving past that to ask if there was anything else. She wondered if he was fully awake yet. She nodded to Ander, indicating that he should answer the question since he'd been the one to spot the station.

"No sir," said Ander. "But to be fair, the only way we spotted this was when it came into view of our optics. It's completely dead. Shall I adjust our heading to intercept it?" There was another pause. As it drew out, Ander started to look nervous.

Jill sensed he was second-guessing what had clearly been his assumption that the captain would want to change course to investigate. "If you want, I can plot a course to give it a wider berth and avoid it completely," he continued after Spear didn't answer.

"No," the captain finally said, "That's quite alright. We really should check it out if we're going to claim our stake here. Besides, I am as curious as I suspect you are. What is our ETA?" His tone assumed a more reassuring quality. The hesitance from a moment before vanished.

"Two hours and thirty-two minutes," said Ander.

"Very good, I'll be back up there shortly. Spear out"

* * *

Sara-Jay Schieva stepped into the cargo bay to find most of her mining team already assembled. The celebratory vibe from earlier was still there but tempered by the anticipation of hard work to come. She joined two of her team members who stood together. There were seven teams of four, one for each of the mining shuttles docked neatly in a row overhanging the chasm of the cargo hold. The individual teams stood grouped together on the upper level, talking and waiting for the meeting to start.

"Where's Ava?" asked Sara-Jay. Ava, the fourth member of her team, should be here by now. It was almost time to start. Her mining mechanic just pointed with his head over to where shuttle one's team was standing. Tom Hepner, a tall man in his late thirties, was their leader. He stood near his team talking with Ava. Sara-Jay couldn't make out any of the words in the general clamor of conversation that was echoing off the walls, but their body language was suggestive. She keyed her com unit.

"Ava, we're assembling for the departure briefing," she said. Ava turned from Tom and looked in her direction. Sara-Jay waived. Ava gave Tom an exaggerated shrug and walked over to join them. Before she made it back, Gus Masterson, the Chief of Mining Operations aboard the Philosopher King, stepped into the center of the group and motioned for quiet.

"Okay," he said. His voice was loud and gruff, and it brought the last of the lingering conversation to a halt. "I know you're all excited about what the sensors are saying. I am too, but we all know that no one gets paid until the work is done. We're professionals and we will tackle this just like any other job."

Sara-Jay hadn't worked with Gus before, but he was somewhat of a legend in the prospecting industry. He'd worked for more outfits than she could name over a career that spanned decades. He brought his data slate up and pointed at it. Sara-Jay looked at her own and could see that an operational plan and set of objectives had loaded onto the screen.

"Most of you are going to deploy now and begin setting up shop on the asteroids," said Gus. "Shuttle team leaders three through seven, I have marked your target asteroids on your individual-objectives summary. Team leaders one and two, you will set up base on the third planet's alpha moon. Establish factory and refinery infrastructure to build what we need and process what the other teams bring in from the asteroids." The third planet had two moons, one considerably larger than the other. Gus had tagged the larger one "alpha" and the smaller one "beta."

An airless moon was always better than a planet for centralizing operations owing to its far smaller gravity well and lack of disruptive weather. Shuttles and material barges could drop off their payloads using much less fuel. For similar reasons, asteroids were more efficient to mine if they contained the desired material. The ones in this system appeared to have it in abundance.

"Teams one and two, work together to get things set up quickly," Gus said. "I want the equipment up and running when the first material comes in from the asteroids. Also, I'd like at least one of you to take a shuttle down to the planet and do some scouting. There's no way in *vacuum* that we'll be able to mine anything down there on this trip, but the boss will want some close-up scans to show investors for the follow-up mission." He paused and looked down at his notes one last time before asking, "Any questions?" There were none. "Then head 'em up, and move'em out!" he shouted.

The mining crews scrambled to their shuttles.

Sara-Jay and her team boarded mining shuttle two via the large rear hatch. She followed Ava into the cockpit and strapped into the co-pilot's chair as the other woman went through the preflight checklist. The other two team members strapped into chairs in the rear compartment alongside the equipment they had loaded earlier.

Each shuttle contained the beginnings of an automated refinery and a mobile extraction auger. The completed versions of each of these machines would be considerably larger than the shuttles themselves and impractical to haul, so nano assemblers were used to build the rest of the machines from raw materials at the mining site. This way, only certain parts that were beyond the nano assemblers' capabilities had to be packed and transported. Everything else would be built on demand, including living quarters.

Sara-Jay looked at Ava. The preflight checklist was complete now but neither had said a word to the other. Sara-Jay felt the need to clear the air.

"So," Sara-Jay said. "Are you excited about the star system? If it pans out like they're saying, our shares in the stake should make us all rich."

Ava turned her head slowly and looked at Sara-Jay appraisingly.

"Being rich isn't all it's cracked up to be," she said while adopting a smile that struck Sara-Jay as just a little condescending.

"You would know?" Sara-Jay asked, not quite keeping sudden annoyance from creeping into her voice.

Ava's smile brightened at that. "I might, boss."

There was an awkward silence then. Sara-Jay was still trying to come up with a response when the captain's voice cut in over the com.

"Philosopher King to mining shuttles, you are clear for departure."

The giant cargo bay doors parted, opening up the great belly of the Philosopher King from which the small fleet of mining shuttles streamed out. Five of them flared their engines and soared off to the asteroid belt while two dropped into the gravity well of the third planet and raced after her moon. It was time to harvest the motherlode.

* * *

"Wow," Spear said as he stepped out onto the bridge.

"I know, right?" said Ander.

"I don't recall seeing anything like that in the database. Do we have any idea how old it is?" asked Spear.

"No, I've checked our local datastream, and I was about to

send out a deep space query," said Jill.

They went silent for a long moment, mesmerized by the slowly rotating image on the holoscreen.

"I can transmit a query to deep space relay fourteen," Phil prompted. "The expected minimum response time will be seven days, four hours, and twenty-six minutes."

"That's okay, Phil," said the captain. "I think it's unlikely that we'll find anything on the mainstream about this region of space that we haven't already downloaded." He looked around the bridge. "So what do we think about it? Is this some long-lost relic from a long-dead civilization, or something more recent?"

Once Spear had seen the space station, as weird as it was, it reassured him since it was nothing like what he and his brother had run across in the Beta Adonis system. He felt his sense of adventure coming back. He hadn't felt that in a long time, and it was invigorating.

"We really don't know anything," said Jill. "Space has a way of preserving things, so it could have been abandoned twenty years ago or two thousand and we just wouldn't know without a closer inspection."

"And by closer inspection, you mean that we should stop in and take a look." Spear didn't pause for an answer. "Ander, is there any way we could dock with that thing?"

"It has some really large features around the outer perimeter that appear to be hangar bay doors, but I don't know how we would open them," said Ander. "There's also a lot of debris floating around so I don't think we should bring the ship too close. I suggest we take up a relative position about seven thousand meters off the station and send in a shuttle. If we were somehow able to get those doors open and clear some of the debris, we might be able to dock."

"Assuming those are indeed hangars and that they're not already full up," said Spear.

"I think we should also make sure we can keep the doors open," said Jill.

"Good point," said Spear. "It looks like an interesting place to visit, but I'd hate to have to set up long-term residence." He then addressed the ship. "Phil, would you please page Maxwell and ask him to come to the bridge?"

A few minutes later, the hatch in the rear of the bridge opened and Maxwell Forrester, the ship's security chief, stepped out. He was a muscular, broad-shouldered man with short-cropped gray hair and a face that was all hard angles. There was no softness in his features, but his bright green eyes conveyed a disarming congeniality at times. Right now, though, they were hooded as they took in the bridge. He recognized what looked vaguely like a giant space station of some sort dominating the main holoscreen.

The captain spun on his heel to face Maxwell while adopting a bright cheery smile that Maxwell knew was meant to annoy him. Maxwell had known the captain back when Spear was still a spunky youth working for his older brother. While time and tragedy had layered on some quiet maturity, the captain still seemed to enjoy ribbing him from time to time with some pointed levity. What Spear didn't know, and what Maxwell wasn't about to let him find out, was that time had done the opposite to himself. Down deep, Maxwell was not quite the hard-boiled military soul he had once been, but he liked to maintain the facade.

"Maxwell!" Spear said. "Just the man I wanted to see!" Maxwell remained motionless. He looked at Ander and Jill who had also turned to face him and then back again at the image on the holoscreen. Phil hadn't informed him as to *why* he'd been summoned to the bridge, but his mind was quick. It had to be to survive twenty years in the Star Navy Marine Corps. Given what had obviously been occupying the entire bridge crew's attention prior to his entrance, it was no mystery to Maxwell what he was about to be asked to do. Even before the captain opened his mouth again to continue, Maxwell knew he'd be leading a team over to whatever in God's bright universe that thing was on the screen. He decided to just take it head-on.

"I'll take a four-man team in full dive gear," Maxwell said, beating Spear to the point. "We can be ready to go in thirty minutes."

Spear closed his mouth, his request now unnecessary. He smiled again appraisingly. "That's what I like about you Maxwell, you're always one step ahead of me."

CHAPTER 4

The small transport shuttle detached from the bottom of the Philosopher King's hull where it normally hung hidden along the sleek underbelly. Once the small vessel was fifteen meters away from the hull, its main thrusters lit up briefly and expended just enough reaction mass to place it on its course toward the derelict space station. Outer blast shields lowered at the front of the cockpit allowing occupants to see outside through the transparent aluminum windows that surrounded the pilot's chair in an arc.

Maxwell stared as the space station consumed the view at this close range, catching the glint of an occasional piece of debris darting past them as they traveled inbound. Joe Schieva was at the controls. Maxwell and one other dive team member hovered over his shoulders trying to get a look at the monstrosity. The shuttle had three main compartments, including the cockpit and a common area behind it, which contained a table, some couches, and a galley. A tiny cargo bay was in the rear, as well as the lift doors through which Maxwell and his team had emerged a few minutes earlier. The lift deposited them in the shuttle and then retreated back into the King before the smaller ship detached.

Three other dive team members were in the common compartment readying a portable plasma torch for burning into the station. Maxwell noticed Joe was having to work the controls ever more deftly as they neared the station and the debris field got denser. He leaned over to Jax Dyson, his second in command, who was the other team member staring out the windows. Maxwell whispered, so as not to distract their pilot.

"What do you think?"

Jax considered for a long moment. The light reflecting off the station gave his dark skin an eerie tone and made his eyes seem to glow. Jax was tall like Maxwell, but where Maxwell was broad-shouldered and a little stocky, Jax was lean and lanky. Where Maxwell sported a short military-style haircut, Jax had long dreadlocks that slinked down his shoulders front and back. His long facial features didn't seem to register his boss's question, but there was an almost imperceptible lift of his right eyebrow. Maxwell saw it. In what seemed a lifetime ago they had served together in the navy and had maintained a friendship forged under fire. Maxwell was used to his friend's minimalist reactions.

"I think we cut a hole large enough to get us and the torch through and use the diving harnesses for maneuvering, and take it slow," Jax finally said. After the navy, Jax had spent years salvaging derelicts and recovering remains and valuables from abandoned wrecks. He had more experience diving into the unknown than all of Maxwell's other team, including himself, combined. "It seems likely to me that a structure this large will have some room to move about, especially if Navarro's right about it being a hangar of some kind, but it could just as easily be as tight as a rabbit warren in there." Maxwell nodded his head and turned back to the forward view. Schieva was making his final approach.

The small craft pivoted as it neared the outer hull of the space station allowing its upper bulkhead to become parallel to the structure. Schieva nudged the controls, slowing them down to a velocity of mere centimeters per second before activating the docking clamps, which reached out the final half meter and locked onto the station using powerful magnetic seals. Unlike docking with the Philosopher King, there was no neat, perfectly shaped groove in the side of the space station for the shuttle to melt into, but both the clamps and a manual port hatch were designed to extend outward and accommodate docking with irregular points of ingress.

Once the clamps were secure, Maxwell's team suited up. They decompressed the main commons compartment since there was no expectation of a breathable atmosphere inside the structure. Joe Schieva remained in the now-sealed cockpit with atmosphere while the others carefully positioned the cutting torch, pointing it upward at the ceiling hatch, which was presently opened. The torch executed a circular cutting pattern just smaller than the radius of the hatch with two swirling plasma beams. In the center, the torch had a singular shaft extending upwards to hold and then extract the center piece once the hole was complete. Tiny pieces of particulate from the station's hull swirled around suited figures as the torch bit deeper and deeper. Finally, the whirling light show stopped when the torch detected it had cut all the way through. The arm distended, holding the removed-section like a plate and leaving a round hole in its place.

The team, led by Jax Dyson, floated through the hatch and newly cut aperture one by one. Once through the opening, each team member planted their feet onto the inner side of the station's hull and reactivated their magnetic boots to keep from floating off. Once he was through, Maxwell took a moment to look around the gigantic chamber in which they found themselves. He shined the penetrating lights from his suit into the darkness. The room was so large the beams disappeared in the distance before illuminating the far wall. He switched to infrared on his helmet's heads-up display. His team members now appeared as blotchy orange figures, each tagged with their name, as his sensors picked up the heat emanating from their suits.

"Well, it looks to me that Navarro was right," Maxwell said over the com. "This definitely fits the bill for a hanger bay of some sort."

"I agree," said Jax. "I'm measuring it at just over a million cubic meters. That's enough area to stow a small fleet."

"And," said Maxwell, "this is one of six such structures on this station. Are there any ships docked?" A moment later an answer came over the com system.

"I think I've got something, sir." Maxwell recognized the voice as belonging to Will Shoemaker, one of his junior security officers. Shoemaker pointed a green laser at something floating in a corner, up and at an angle from where they stood. "It might be a vessel of some kind. It's about the size of a mining shuttle and seems to be drifting independently of the station. Permission to investigate?"

Maxwell looked at Jax.

"I'll go with him," Jax said, returning Maxwell's glance and then turning to look up at the object. "Okay Will, on my lead. Unlock boots and give a two-second hydrogen boost."

The two shot up from the "floor" of the giant room releasing tiny jets of hydrogen gas to propel them through the vacuum up toward their destination. They flew quickly, and Maxwell could see them reorient midway, releasing quick bursts to slow their momentum as they approached.

"Sir." Another voice grabbed Maxwell's attention. "We think we have a hatch over here. It may be an access point into the station proper."

Maxwell turned and walked over to where two of his men stood next to a large octagonal structure. They had attached sensors to the thing, and he could see that the readouts were registering a faint pressure on the other side. He could also make out seams in the supposed hatch projecting from each corner and meeting in the center. His intuition told him that this was where the door parted. It was large, about four meters in width. He could imagine support vehicles going in and out of it to service or tow ships. Just then, the captain's voice came over the com.

"What have we got, Maxwell?" he said.

"Looks like Navarro was right, at least about the docking bays. Some of my guys think they might have even found a small vessel. Right now, I'm staring at what appears to be a hatch to the rest of the station. We're detecting some faint pressure on the other side, and we think it's atmosphere."

After a short delay, the captain said, "Very good! Any idea about this thing's origin?"

"I'm a soldier, not an archaeologist. You'll need to send over some of the brain trust to find that out."

Suddenly, Maxwell staggered, as a wave of pressure buffeted him. It would have knocked him over had his magnetic boots not held him in place. As he recovered and looked around, he could see that one of his men *had* fallen over and the large hatch was now standing wide open.

"Maxwell, are you still there?" the captain asked with concern creeping into his voice.

"Yes, Captain, I am still here, and we are okay. I think one of my boys just inadvertently triggered an airlock." Through the now open hatch, Maxwell could see that the inside was an octagonal chamber that extended a few meters before terminating in another identical octagonal hatch. He was also a little angry that his team hadn't been more careful or at least *warned* him before they started punching buttons or pulling levers.

"What happened?" he barked into the com. One of his men, the one who had fallen over, began speaking while managing to look sheepish even through the envirosuit.

"I think I found the manual release," he said.

Twenty minutes later, Maxwell and his team had managed to identify the manual actuators for both the inner and outer hatches. The two hatches appeared to be an airlock. But with no power to cycle it, they were careful to close the outer door to the hangar before opening the inner one to preserve as much of the remaining atmosphere as possible in the station beyond. Not that it was breathable. It was far too high on concentrations of carbon dioxide for starters, and even a few other gasses that his envirosuit told him would be fatal if inhaled. Nonetheless, the tech guys on the King had wanted them to preserve it in case there was operational equipment inside that might not be hardened for vacuum.

When Maxwell asked about the dangerous gasses he detected, the consensus was that it had probably become contaminated over time. Only Ander Navarro had suggested, "Maybe that's what the aliens breathe."

Maxwell hadn't checked in on Jax and Shoemaker, being so busy with the airlock, and they hadn't reported in. He wasn't worried yet because he trusted Jax's skills and experience, but he had just triggered the com when he heard Shoemaker's voice.

"Hey boss, checking in," the man said.

"Shoemaker, good to hear from you. You've been quiet. Where's Jax?"

"Yeah, sorry boss, it's definitely a ship of some kind up here. Jax found a way in, but it seems to block our com signal. He's still looking around inside, and man, it's weird. He sent me out to check in."

"Roger that," Maxwell said. "Just proceed with caution and check in again in twenty minutes if Jax isn't done yet." Maxwell could imagine that a ship of unknown origin would certainly pique the interest of a long-time derelict diver like Jax. He would want him back eventually to help explore the rest of the station, but so far, they'd just been exploring an empty corridor. They were waiting for a team of tech heads to be shuttled over from the King, now that they'd secured the airlock, and were reasonably sure that there was no immediate threat. He could give Jax a little more time.

* * *

Jax made his way cautiously into the strange spacecraft. He had seen abandoned vessels of virtually every conceivable make and model spanning the last couple of centuries of human space travel, but he'd never seen anything like this. It was a small vessel composed of four main compartments and a corridor along the outer bulkhead providing access to all of them. But unlike most of the ships Jax had explored, everything seemed neat and near pristine. He imagined that if he touched the right buttons or flipped the right switches the thing might well come to life. That is, if there had been any buttons or switches in sight. The fact was, he hadn't seen anything that looked like a control panel or even a display screen in the twenty minutes he had been floating around the ship.

He'd sent Shoemaker out the hatch to check in with the boss, but he found he was having trouble tearing himself away from the strange vessel. In addition to the lack of obvious control or display apparatuses, the proportions of everything seemed off. There were a large number of spaceship makers, ranging from government contractors to commercial civilian companies and innumerable different designs and classes, but basic human anatomy dictated certain dimensions and arrangements that could be recognized in any ship, except this one.

A few items floated around freely, but Jax figured most of the loose items were stowed away in what appeared to be lockers and compartments lining the walls of the outer corridor. One feature, however, repeated itself frequently enough for Jax to take notice: colored spheres standing atop thin pedestals that protruded from various angles throughout the ship. Jax paused in front of a red one in the room farthest from the hatch through which he had entered.

This orb was larger than the other ones, and he found himself transfixed before it. One of his dreadlocks slipped in front of his left eye in his helmet, and he shifted his head to get it out of the way. The object appeared inert like the rest of the ship, not glowing or illuminated in any way but shiny, and he appreciated the fish-eye reflection of his helmet on its surface. He waved his mobile scanner over it. Just like everything else in the ship, it betrayed no trace of radiation or thermal signature. And like the ship itself, it was beautiful for its simplicity.

As Jax stood there, his thoughts wandered past the object

before him and back to the vessel as a whole. All aspects of it were spartan and uncluttered in design. This lent it an efficient elegance that appealed to Jax's sensibilities. His hand moved toward the cantaloupe-sized sphere. It was a shame that such a ship had sat here dormant for so long. Such engineering and design should be put to use, employed in the simple business of space travel, not locked away in this dead wreck of a space station.

He should fly this ship. The thought came suddenly. He should take it out and let it be useful again. It was form coupled tightly to function. It was beautiful, and the welcoming warmth from the now-glowing spheroid device sent a certain reassurance through him as his gloved hand grasped it.

Then with a sudden jolt, Jax's eyes snapped back open as the ship lurched from its station and sent him careening into the bulkhead. The lights from his envirosuit winked out as a cold chill ran through his body. He checked his helmet's heads-up display even as he felt the ship continue to accelerate around him. The display lit up weakly and flickered. His battery was almost completely drained.

Two concerns now raced through Jax's mind and fought for dominance. The first was the knowledge that the ship was moving and would be very shortly crashing into an outer hangar wall. The second was that without any power, his envirosuit wouldn't be able to scrub the carbon dioxide from his atmosphere or keep him warm enough to survive for very long. Ultimately, the former concern won out as it had more immediate consequences. Then, just as suddenly as it started, the ship stopped its acceleration, and he was no longer pressed against the wall. Jax knew he was still moving, still careening for an outer wall and a nasty crash, but at least whatever thruster or form of locomotion that had launched the ship from its ancient repose had disengaged. Without another thought, Jax bolted from the room grabbing whatever handholds he could find to push himself through the corridor, carefully avoiding touching any of the other spheroid apparatuses. Finally, he found the open hatch and launched himself out of it.

As he exited, Jax reached down and flipped the manual switch on his micro-booster expelling reaction mass to neutralize his momentum. The strange vessel fell away below him, getting smaller and smaller until finally, he saw it strike and then bounce off the far wall. It tumbled and spun. Jax thought he could see some minor debris fly off of it as it gyrated through the hanger bay, not stopping until it finally became entangled in some cabling.

Jax looked and could see other team members scrambling. They were beside what appeared to be a large access hatch. Fortunately, they hadn't been in the path of the errant ship. He glanced up as a flash of light caught his eye. It was Shoemaker. He'd just lit off his own micro-booster and was coming to intercept Jax. Jax was relieved. Shoemaker was okay too. He was also sure that they were trying to raise him over the com and wondering why he wasn't responding. But his suit was completely dead now. No matter, he'd be all right long enough for them to get him into the shuttle's airlock. Jax waved to Shoemaker as he approached to let him know he wasn't injured. What he didn't know was how he was going to tell Maxwell why in God's vast space he had touched that thing in the ship. He didn't even know how to explain it to himself.

CHAPTER 5

Ander Navarro could hardly contain his excitement on the shuttle ride over to the space station. He'd been thrilled to find out that he'd been right about the large structures being hangar bays. It had been little more than a lucky guess, but the confirmation made him feel like he understood the builders on some basic level. And now here he was, on his way to investigate the "alien" space station. Deep down, he didn't really believe it was an alien structure in the "little green men" sense. Ander suspected that this was some long-forgotten outpost of humanity. Such things did exist and were found from time to time along the frontier zones. Nevertheless, his facetious talk about aliens had caught on and many of the crew now speculated about what they might look like or how many eyes or legs they might have. There weren't any deep theoretical scientist types on the ship who could've offered an educated opinion. This was primarily a profit-seeking venture, so the engineers were the closest thing they had. Only when his com buzzed was he reminded of the other preeminent scientific mind on the ship.

"Are we there yet?" The attempt at humor from the ship's synthetic intelligence caused Ander to roll his eyes.

"Hello Phil, I suppose you are as anxious as the rest of us to see what is inside this thing."

"That's right. Your idea of this being an alien artifact still only yields a probability of 0.23 percent, but that's up 0.03 percent from where it was before we boarded the station. Still, I am eager to see if you are correct."

"For the record," Ander said, "I am not *predicting* that it's aliens, I just think that we should be open to the possibility."

"Of course," said Phil, "My mistake."

"Are you going to be disappointed if it's not aliens?" Ander asked.

"Yes and no," said Phil. "On the one hand, discovering this to be a heretofore undocumented human settlement would bring to an end several scenario simulations I am currently running based on the speculation that it is aliens. But on the other hand, it would open up an entirely new line of historical inquiry into humanity's diaspora into space."

Ander was learning that these "scenario simulations" that Phil mentioned at times must be what passed for an imagination for him. He was about to say more when he felt the subtle thud of the shuttle docking with the makeshift hatch that Maxwell and his team had installed on the side of the station.

"Are we there yet?" Phil asked again.

"Yes," Ander said. "We are most definitely there."

* * *

Crawling into the hangar bay from the shuttle, Ander could see the dive team had been at work setting up lights and markers to make sense of the place. Several items outside the immediate vicinity of the shuttle hatch were tagged with electronic markers.

They were designed to interact with his envirosuit's helmet. If he paused for a second on a particular item, a display would pop up with notes from the team. One object, a little ways off, caught his attention. It was the hull of a small ship that one of the dive team members had accidentally activated and sent careening through the cavernous space. He heard about the incident just before coming over from the King, but the details were still murky. A virtual tag highlighted streaks along the ship's side where it had scraped against the hangar, but it seemed otherwise undamaged. The dive team had since identified several other small craft inside the hangar. Unlike this one, which had been adrift, the rest were anchored with docking clamps to the interior.

Ander wanted to go over and take a look for himself, but instead, he joined the rest of the newcomers as they walked along the lighted path to the inner airlock the dive team had figured out how to work. Once through the airlock, Ander and his companions were able to take off their helmets. The dive team had determined that there was very little atmosphere of any kind left in this part of the station and deployed portable life-support units. The units, which filtered out any lingering harmful gasses or particulates, glowed bright green to indicate the air was now safe to breathe. This section of the station consisted of a large corridor, about one hundred meters long, and several chambers immediately off it. There was another large hatch at the far end of the corridor, similar to the one through which he had just come. Maxwell had locked that one down to ensure no one accidentally opened it and depressurized the area.

Ander walked along the mainly featureless corridor carrying a handheld uplink unit that extended the Philosopher King's network, and thereby Phil, into the station. There were twelve rooms in the pressurized section, all toward the interior. Their hatches were open, and Ander peered into each one to his right as he passed. Without artificial gravity, his magnetic boots tethered him with each step. Ander made a complete circuit before returning to the largest of the rooms and entering it. Inside, he found two engineers recording everything.

The room was filled with colored spheres of various sizes suspended on cylindrical pedestals jutting out from all directions. To Ander's eye, everything was just a little off. The proportions and placement of items in the room seemed wrong somehow, unnatural. Phil was being silent, but he knew the synthetic intelligence was busy recording and analyzing everything. No doubt Phil was running more simulations. Ander's eyes focused on a large green sphere resting on its pedestal in the direct center of the room. It was almost a meter in diameter and something about it captured his focus.

Ander drew closer, contemplative. Something about this one seemed different to him—but not just because it was the largest and most centrally located one. The quiet conversation among the engineers faded from his awareness as he stared. Was Ander imagining things or was it glowing, just slightly? The sphere began to fill his field of vision as he inched closer, and yes, it was glowing slightly, he was sure now, a definite...

A large, gloved hand latched onto his wrist. Ander's awareness came rushing back to him. His hand was frozen now with his fingers just centimeters from the sphere. The engineers had stopped talking and were looking at him. He heard Phil over uplink calling his name, and following the arm attached to the hand that now restrained his, he met the penetrating eyes of Jax Dyson. He blinked and pulled his hand back. Jax released his wrist.

"Ander Navarro!" he heard Phil saying, "Are you alright?" Ander looked down at the uplink and then back up at Jax.

"He is now," the larger man said, not taking his gaze off Ander.

"What... what happened?" Ander managed.

"Your envirosuit indicated that your heart rate had elevated suddenly, and you became unresponsive," Phil said. "Then I noticed you seemed to be moving toward the unidentified interface. I alerted the rest of the crew in your vicinity. I don't think you should be touching the interfaces until we understand them better."

Ander was lost. "The interfaces?" he asked.

"Yes," said Jax. Jax hadn't been in the room when Ander entered. He learned later that Jax was passing by the opening when Phil sent the alert. Jax's leaping stride had carried him to Ander before anyone else reacted, and he had still just barely caught Ander's hand before it touched the sphere. "I touched one of these in a vessel that was floating in the hangar. I activated the ship. It is an interface of some kind." Ander blinked with realization.

"Did it speak to you?" Jax asked.

"Wha...what? Speak?" Ander was struggling to catch up.

"Did you feel drawn to it?" Jax asked. Ander thought for a moment, still trying to clear his head. He hadn't *intended* to touch the sphere. There had been a note from the dive team that specifically implored them to not touch things. He didn't remember lifting his hand, but he did remember being strangely captivated by it.

"Yes," he said at length. "It seemed like it was glowing."

"I detected no increase in luminosity," said Phil.

"Yes," Jax said, "I saw it too, when I was on the ship."

"So, you're the one who crashed it?" Ander asked unnecessarily. Jax stared at him. "... er that is, you're the one who discovered that these things are control interfaces of some sort?"

Jax grunted and turned to leave the room.

"Thanks, by the way," Ander called after him. If Jax heard him, he didn't show it as he disappeared into the corridor.

"Friendly, that chap," said Phil from the uplink. "I need more data."

Ander looked down at the uplink in his hand. "More data?" he asked.

"Yes, it's apparent to me that both you and Jax Dyson experienced some kind of hallucination after encountering these spheroids, and I'd like someone to bring a portable medical imager from the ship," Phil said.

"To scan someone's brain while they gaze at one of the spheres," Ander said, putting together what kind of experiment Phil wanted to conduct.

"Exactly," Phil said, "care to volunteer?"

* * *

The captain leaned against the bulkhead in the conference room. It was the ship's only conference room, and it would have felt claustrophobic if it weren't for the half ring of rear-facing windows on the other side. Positioned on the spine of the ship, the room's windows offered an impressive view of the Philosopher King's large glowing sub-light engines which pivoted on their pylons as the helm made minor course corrections. A holographic rendering of Ander Navarro from the waist up hovered over the center round table. Jill Thomas and Dr. Alena Ellison stood nearby, also ignoring the conference room's chairs. John Terry and Maxwell Forrester stood at the opposite end in front of the large windows. Navarro spoke and gestured.

"Phil thinks that these spheres are affecting the brain somehow, but we need an imager to capture what exactly is going on while it's happening," Ander said.

Spear watched Dr. Ellison's face as Ander spoke, seeing the growing concern gathering in her dark intelligent eyes. Dr. Ellison was shorter than Jill, with a slight frame that was in sharp contrast to Jill's tall athletic build. Her dark hair was curly and done up in a loose bun. She'd been the last crew member he hired and had only arrived on the ship a few hours before launch. So far, he'd found her to be quiet and contemplative. Dr. Ellison was a newly minted Medicus Practitioner from the Orion Medical Academy. Medical staff were some of the hardest to find, due to their demand, and Spear was grateful he'd been able to hire her, despite her lack of experience. For Dr. Ellison's part, the experience she acquired on this ship would help her earn full doctor status. She would then be free to launch a private practice or join one of the colonial hospital networks. He knew this was the reason she'd signed on. It was a mutually beneficial arrangement.

"This does not sound like a good idea," Dr. Ellison said as the dam holding back her objections finally broke. "We have no idea what the alien spheres are doing to your brain and what the long-term effects of exposure might be. Also, beyond the physiological, the symptoms you described sound almost like some sort of hypnosis. We don't know what psychological consequences there might be."

"Which is why we need to run some tests, to find out what these things are doing," Ander said. "Look, Jax and I have already been exposed, and I'm willing to give it another go to see what we can learn."

"For science...," Jill said with not a little sarcasm creeping into her voice. It was not lost on Spear that the casual mention of aliens was no longer drawing skepticism. Could this really be a first-contact situation? That would certainly make waves back home and probably confirm their place in the history books.

"Look," said Ander, "I think these things, whatever they are, are trying to interact with us somehow. So far, all other investigation has yielded little that we didn't already know. There are no displays, no writings we can translate, not even a lever or a button in any of the areas we've explored. This may be our only way of learning who built this thing and who lived in this star system."

"In any of the areas we've explored so far, Ander," Jill said. "We've only covered a fraction of the station. It may be that there are plenty of books, screens, and levers in other sections."

Jill glanced over at Spear who returned her gaze blankly. The truth was, every fiber in Spear's being wanted to be over there trying it out himself. Up until the discovery of the strange hypnotic spheres, he'd been convinced that this was just some long-abandoned colony that had somehow been lost to history. But now, the natural explorer in him was clawing to get out and discover whatever fantastically weird secrets this station, and ultimately this entire star system had to offer.

"Captain?" Spear looked up to see five pairs of eyes, one holographic, staring at him. It was Jill who had addressed him. He straightened up.

"Ander," he began. "Are you sure you want to do this? You

would be taking a significant risk."

"I am," Ander said.

"What about the station?" Spear asked. "Is there any danger of it careening off like the small ship in the hangar bay did when Jax activated it?"

"Not a chance," Ander said. "There's just not enough energy available. We think the small ship tapped Jax's envirosuit for energy, and even then, only engaged a split-second burst of thrust. The entire Philosopher King doesn't have the energy necessary to move this station."

The idea of the station draining his ship of energy was not a comforting thought to Spear, but he tucked *that* budding scenario in his mind away for the moment. It was probably just paranoid.

"That's something I wanted to mention," said Maxwell. "I suggest that if we do this, no one touches the thing. That should prevent any power transfer. If it can drain an envirosuit, it might be able to mess up a human pretty bad too given the opportunity."

"Phil?" Spear asked.

"I agree with Chief Forrester's suggestion," Phil said. "Based on Ander Navarro's experience, it is apparent that the interaction does not require physical touch, at least not initially."

Spear glanced back at Dr. Ellison. "Doctor, how opposed are you to this experiment?" he asked.

She was silent for a long moment. "If Ander is willing and understands the danger, then I won't stand in the way. However, I do insist on being present with a full suite of med scanners to monitor his vitals in real-time. If I detect anything happening to him that looks dangerous, we shut it down."

She nodded as she said the last few words. The captain nodded back at her.

"Agreed. Ander, I think we'll give it a go, but not until Dr. Ellison arrives and has her equipment set up. I'm going to come over as well. All this talk of alien technology has finally gotten to me." He looked at Jill sheepishly but she just returned a small smile of her own revealing that even *she* wasn't immune to the excitement.

* * *

It took a few hours for Dr. Ellison, the captain, and the medical equipment to arrive and be set up. Ander was trying to be patient, but he was too excited. Jax Dyson hadn't spoken another word to him since stopping him from touching the sphere, though he popped in periodically to watch the engineers as they continued to study and document the rooms off the main corridor. The dive team had also set up a collapsible airlock at the end of the corridor opposite the hangar and were getting ready to explore the next section along the perimeter of the station.

It was hard to scan through the strange material that the station was made of, but it looked like there were closed hatches at regular intervals that they might be able to open and pressurize incrementally. Maxwell Forrester had directed most of the efforts of the dive team toward that end.

More and more crew members had come over to the station, though the limited capabilities of the one transport shuttle had made that a slow process. Most of them who weren't immediately needed for the task at hand returned after a few hours to limit the stress on the portable life support units and give others the opportunity to visit the station. A few artifacts had been found and carried back for further study, though there weren't many things laying around that could be easily transported. It seemed to Ander that whoever these aliens were, they had been tidy.

"Are you ready?" Dr. Ellison broke into Ander's thoughts as she finished strapping the last of the scanning equipment to his body. She had attached several small sensors to him and set up a monitoring station with a terminal that she could use to track his vital signs and brain activity.

"Yes," he said. "Phil? Are *you* ready?"

"I am," came the disembodied voice.

"Well, here goes nothing," Ander said, giving a final glance over his shoulder at the captain who was standing near the opening, arms crossed. Spear gave him a reassuring nod and he turned once again to gaze into the sphere.

At first, nothing happened. The room fell silent as conversations died. Everyone present was now watching him. Then the sphere once again seemed to take on a sheen. Ander knew from what Phil said earlier that it was probably not giving off actual light, but to him, it certainly did appear to glow. He felt again the urge to reach out and touch it. He doubled down on his resolve to remain still, consciously forcing his hands to remain at his sides. The sphere still beckoned him, but it wasn't overpowering. He found he could still exercise his will. That, at least, was reassuring. He spared a sideways glance at the doctor, but she was carefully studying her display.

A few more seconds passed. The sphere still glowed and beckoned, but nothing more. He felt like he was on the verge of unlocking something, but he didn't know how to turn the key. Ander knew he shouldn't touch the thing. He agreed that would be too dangerous given Jax Dyson's experience, but that was precisely what it seemed to want him to do. Then he had another thought. This had to be some kind of neural interface since it was obviously affecting his mind and making him see things. Perhaps this operated on a similar principle to a ship's drive interface. When piloting, he wore a headset that touched his temples and fed raw data from the ship's sensors into his nervous system. Ander had been trained to allow the information to flow through his consciousness and let it build a mental picture of the surrounding region of hyperdimensional space that he could navigate by. The effectiveness of this technique was equal parts learned skill and natural talent, sort of like playing a musical instrument. Ander had been among the most skilled and talented in his graduating class. This thing was already transmitting something into his mind so maybe he just needed to let it build him a picture.

He decided to put his hypothesis to the test. Summoning the same techniques he used when interfacing with the shadow drive, he let his perceptions relax and broaden. He opened up his mind to incoming data and images. He felt a reaction, like a switch had flipped on in his mind. There was something familiar about it. Whatever the sphere was doing, he could now tell that it was indeed operating on similar principles to a drive interface, but different in flavor and far stronger.

A bright burst of light sent Ander reeling from the sphere and stumbling to the floor—or at least, he *thought* it sent him reeling. As he got up, he was shocked to see his own body still standing in front of the sphere, motionless. He turned his head to survey the room. Everyone else who had been present was still there, also standing as if frozen, and still looking at his standing form. The doctor looked as if she might be in the act of raising her head to look up from her display. Ander got to his feet and then took a rather surreal stroll around himself. The air held a stuffy quality, and the sphere glowed brilliantly. He stared at his own eyes, which were focused forward.

"Oh, God," Ander mouthed. "What's going on here?"

"Three," a voice echoed through the room. Ander, or at least his now out-of-body form, nearly leaped out of its ethereal skin. He looked around. "Three," the voice came again. It seemed to be emanating from the sphere itself. "Three." What did *that* mean? And then the sphere seemed to grow and contort. Ander watched it as it morphed until he recognized the shape of the space station itself. It paused then for a few seconds glowing, a slowly rotating three-dimensional model of the station. Then, the outer hull began to dissolve, revealing a network of corridors and rooms. The meaning was not lost on Ander. Their sensors had been able to do a partial map of the main passageways, but this was far more complete and far more detailed. And then, as he watched, a medium-sized room just off the center of the core of the station, not far from the top as it was oriented, began to pulsate and glow brighter than the rest. Ander stepped closer and peered at the location indicated. He was still considering when the sphere flashed, his eyes blinked, and he found himself once again standing in front of the sphere. Everyone in the room was in motion again. The out-of-body trip had come to an abrupt end.

* * *

"What happened?" Captain Spear asked, grasping Ander's arm firmly to steady him. Ander wavered on his feet when he came back to himself. Spear's eye's shifted from him to Dr. Ellison, imploring one of them to answer his question. Ander was still not responding in full sentences, so the doctor answered first.

"I'm not sure," she said, looking back down at her readings. "It looks like the instruments recorded a significant spike in activity in his cortex, but it only lasted for a split second. His vitals are steady, though his blood pressure increased—but not dangerously so. I'm also detecting a mild rush of adrenaline in his bloodstream, but it's dissipating now."

She looked back up at Spear and then Ander who had now steadied himself. Ander looked at the captain.

"I'm all right," he said. "The transition was just jolting, like waking up suddenly from a dream."

"The transition?" Spear asked. "What are you talking about? What did you experience?"

"Well," Ander said. "It was like I was dreaming, but I was awake, like a lucid dream I guess." He proceeded to relate his out-of-body experience to the captain, the doctor, and the various crew members who had assembled to watch the experiment. Maxwell Forrester was among the audience and spoke up when Ander had finished.

"You say it looked like a map of the station?" he asked. "And that a section was highlighted? Could you point out that section on a schematic constructed from sensor data?"

"Yes," said Ander, "I'm confident I can. It was so vivid, so real."

"Nonetheless," said Spear, "we should probably get you to point it out sooner rather than later while it's still fresh in your mind. Doctor, he only interacted with the sphere for what, less than a second total? How did he have time to see all of this?"

"In a dream state, and what Mr. Navarro is describing does sound like some kind of lucid dream, the brain can compress experiences so that we perceive what seems to be the passage of a large span of time within what in reality are mere moments, or seconds. It's speculated that some people live out the equivalent of years, or even a lifetime, while dreaming in only a matter of moments. That would correspond with the elevated activity in his brain's cortex. I've still got a lot of data to look at, but from what I can tell, it looks like the sphere device initiated a dream or trance-like state in him, but only just briefly. I'm going to look through all of the readings with a fine-tooth comb. I'll put a report together for you."

"Doctor," Phil's voice came over the uplink. "I noticed something about the brain imaging that you may find pertinent."

"Yes, Phil," said Spear. "I was just about to ask you if the ship's sensors had detected any changes in the station's energy state when Ander activated the sphere."

"No sir," said Phil. "Though the ship's sensors don't penetrate the hull of the station very well. It's very possible a small energy signature could have been missed."

Well, thought Spear, *at least the station hadn't gone careening out of place like the ship in the hangar.*

"What did you notice about the brain readings, Philosopher King?" Dr. Ellison asked even as she began to recanvas the readings herself.

"I'm not a medical expert," said Phil. "But as a ship's intelligence I've studied the data and theory concerning a pilot's ability to navigate higher dimensional space while interfaced with the shadow drive system. The consensus is that most pilots, particularly of class three and higher show increased neural activity in a specific region along the anterior of the frontal cortex."

"Yes," said the doctor. "I see it now, that's interesting. The Philosopher King is correct, that particular region of Mr. Navarro's brain was significantly more active during the time he was engaged with the sphere. In fact, that region was more active than any other part. If I didn't know better, I'd think I was looking at a pilot mid-flight between star systems. Good catch."

"Thank you," Phil said.

"Yes, that's right," said Ander. "I knew I couldn't reach out and touch the sphere, so I tried to connect with it the same way I connect to the shadow drive. That seemed to be what really triggered the experience. I think that's the way you're *supposed* to connect to it. It even felt similar at first."

"What does that mean?" asked the captain.

"I think that whatever this interface is, it works on hyper-dimensional principles similar to our shadow drive," said the doctor. "Only, instead of providing a simple representation of shadow space, it connects directly and interactively with the brain."

"An interactive neural interface," Spear said.

"Yes, maybe similar to the ones used for medical prosthetics, but I've never heard of one able to interact with this part of the brain and engage at this level. Captain, whoever built this is at least decades beyond any tech I'm familiar with, maybe more than that."

There was a long silent pause. If there had been any remaining doubt in anyone's mind that they were dealing with alien technology, it now dissolved completely. The implications of what they'd found, the possibilities of this technology, it all weighed heavily in the air. Spear turned back to his security chief.

"Maxwell, get Mr. Navarro a schematic," Spear said. "I want to know what's so important that an ancient telepathic computer drew a map for us."

CHAPTER 6

Rather than trying to work their way through the station to get to the room Ander Navarro had indicated on the schematic, the engineers decided it was easier and quicker to access it via another large room closer to the spot. This room wasn't one of the large hangar bays, but its size and shape indicated that it may have been a cargo hold of some sort. It was only fifty meters away from the room in question and provided easy access once the dive team cut another entrance and set up another airlock for docking. The captain and Dr. Ellison accompanied Ander to the new location via the transport shuttle once atmosphere was established and Maxwell gave the all-clear.

A few hours later, Jill Thomas, who had remained aboard the ship during the previous excursions, came to the station. She wanted to see the place Ander had been directed to in his telepathic vision. She made her way through the new airlock and across the apparent cargo hold, where two members of the dive team were still busy rigging up lights. Finally, Jill stepped into the designated chamber.

The room was about twenty meters across and amazing, simply put. There was no sense of a floor here. The entire chamber was spherical and with their magnetic boots, crew members walked right up the walls and onto the ceiling, recording everything. As she stepped inside, her view was dominated by an explosion of colored spheres in a rainbow of hues ranging in size from a few centimeters to almost a full meter in diameter. They rested atop cylindrical spires that erupted from all sides. There seemed to be a far greater variety of the spheres here than what she'd seen in images from the other part of the station. The room gave Jill the impression that she was at the center of the station's nervous system. This was not in the center of the station's structure, nor was there any evident power source here, but if the station had been an organism, Jill would have labeled *this* its brain.

As an exogeologist, most of this was well outside of her area of expertise. Jill was normally happy to let the engineers do their thing while she toiled away in a corner with her rocks and minerals, but this station had started to profoundly intrigue her. She was after all a scientist at heart, and the one thing that all scientists shared regardless of their respective areas of study was a desire to explore the universe and learn its secrets. She'd initially been very skeptical of this talk of aliens, but while there was still no concrete proof that the structure hadn't been built by human beings, walking into this room was all the convincing she needed. It was alien. It was laid out wrong for humans or any other similar bipedal creature. It did not make sense from that perspective. Design always followed certain rules and made certain assumptions. She was sure now. Whoever built this had a very exotic perspective.

"I wish we had a university research team on board," the captain said, interrupting her thoughts. "We're just not equipped to do this place justice."

Jill had been thinking about that too. "We will have to invite a research team to come to this system, maybe several," she said. "I suspect that there's not an educational institution in all of humanity that won't want a piece of this."

The captain had been staring upward, gazing around the room but now turned to give her a small smile. "It's remarkable isn't it?" he said. "Do you think we're doing the right thing, with Ander's experiments I mean? Should we not just pack up shop and wait for the professionals to get here?"

His comments were sensible. There were others better equipped to handle this kind of thing. But then again, those individuals weren't out here on the fringes of known space, blazing trails. They were tucked comfortably behind their desks drawing faculty salaries.

"I think we are the explorers," she said finally. "We search out far-flung stars hoping to find things that are of value, unique things. This is why we are here. And besides, they'll get their turn. We're here now, we found it, so we have the first claim."

He chuckled and his smile widened.

"Spoken like a true prospector," he said.

* * *

Ander Navarro stood with Maxwell Forrester and Dr. Ellison in the center of the room gazing up at the stalactites of spheres hanging from the ceiling. One large blue sphere loomed in the center suspended by a shaft that was noticeably thicker in proportion to its sphere than the others.

"Well," asked Maxwell, "now that we are here, what are you planning on doing?"

"I suppose the same thing we did before," Ander said. "Pick up the next breadcrumb."

"Philosopher King," said Dr. Ellison, "what do you make of this room?"

The voice over the uplink came after only the slightest pause. "I do not have sufficient data to come to any conclusions, but if I were to speculate, I'd say this is either some sort of systems control hub or maybe even a computer core interface station."

"What makes you think *that*?" asked Maxwell, still gazing at the central artifice.

"There is a much higher density of sphere structures here," said Phil. "If we work on the assumption that these are the actual interfaces aliens would interact with—similar to how humans interact with computer terminals—then a tight clustering would suggest either a centralized operations station of some kind or a place for servicing whatever computer system equivalent controls everything else." No one even batted an eye at the fact that now even the ship's synthetic intelligence was assuming they were dealing with aliens.

"That makes sense," said Maxwell, "but if this is some sort of central operations hub or bridge, won't we be running a risk in interfacing with it? Isn't it possible that doing so will activate something in the station, like automated defenses?"

"I don't think that's the most likely scenario," said Phil. "I've been running over the data with Chief Terry, and we don't see any evidence of active power sources strong enough to move the station or activate a weapons system. Even when Ander interfaced with the other sphere, the ship detected no discernible changes in the station's power state. I'm not saying there are no risks, but activating a large system, like weapons or propulsion, seems like a near impossibility given our dataset."

"Our dataset is what I'm worried about," said Maxwell. "For all we know, these aliens used something for power that we wouldn't even know how to check for."

"Again, a possibility," said Phil. "But so far, the station, as divergent as its design is, seems to be built largely upon engineering concepts we understand and employ in our own structures, with the exception of the spheres."

"With that *one* exception, of course," said Maxwell. He turned to Ander. "Well, should I bother guessing which one of these doohickeys you're planning on mind-talking to?"

"I think," said Ander, "that the big one in the center is the most likely candidate." He glanced back over at the doctor who was still looking up at the large blue sphere. "Careful doctor, it has a way of pulling you in."

She jerked and blinked rapidly, then stared at him for a moment. "Yes," she said, "I think I can appreciate that. I'll need about twenty minutes to set up my gear."

Once the doctor again finished connecting him up to all manner of medical sensors, Ander gazed up at the large blue globe. He felt the draw almost instantly. It was the same pull on his consciousness as before, but even stronger this time. He once again let the data flow into his mind and build the picture. His surroundings became a serene tableau, a fixed frame in time. And as before, he heard the voice say, "Three."

This time, it seemed to come from behind him, rather than from the sphere. He turned to look, or rather his out-of-body-self turned. He was aware of his body, still standing and gazing up at the sphere to his left. He saw something about the size of a tall man. "Three," it spoke again and its shape changed shape constantly.

No, wait, Ander thought. *It's shifting like a ship in shadow space.* He reckoned now that he must somehow be *inside* shadow space and wondered if his own shape too seemed to be shifting. If so, that was outside of his perception. He stared at the apparition.

"Three," he said.

"Three," repeated the form and then added, "you see three, but you can see more."

Then Ander got it.

"You mean three dimensions," Ander said. There was no immediate answer, so he decided to continue. "Greetings, we come in peace." Ander felt only slightly silly saying that. It was cliche from video tales dating back to time immemorial, but it seemed to fit.

"Greetings," replied the form.

Ander felt a rush of excitement. *First contact,* he thought. *I just made first contact!* The creature's tone changed ever so slightly.

"You come to help us," it said. It didn't sound like a question to Ander, just a flat statement like the creature was making a pronouncement.

"Help you?" Ander asked. "What do you mean? How do you know my language?"

"Language is a conveyance," said the thing. "Thoughts are that which is delivered. We know not your language, but your thoughts are plain. You have come to help us."

Ander had no idea what that meant but he felt that he should at the very least try to find out more about this creature.

"Who are you?" Ander asked.

"We are the people," it said. "You have come to our home. But our home is damaged. There are only a few of us." A number was impressed on Ander's consciousness. It wasn't spoken aloud by the creature; he just suddenly knew it. Ten thousand, four hundred, and twenty-four. Ander didn't know how he knew it, but at that moment, he was certain this was the exact number of aliens that still lived. Still lived, a sense of great loss.

There had been more. Billions, perhaps trillions. Ander knew it. This station, the planets, this whole star system had once been teaming with life. He knew it. There was no doubt. Vague images and impressions raced through his mind. A cataclysm, great mourning. Something had happened, something catastrophic.

"What happened to you?" Ander asked, focusing once again on the creature.

"The bright star died," it said. "There was no time to save the people, only a few. We could not travel among the stars as you. We could not run from it. We hid from it instead. Just a few remain. The hiding place grows smaller." The number once again weighed heavily on Ander's mind. "We want to return. We cannot. We need help. The door will not open. It is broken. You have come to open the door."

Then Ander saw the entire station at once, not as a schematic as before but rather the idea of it. The important features of it bore upon him. He knew now that the chamber in which he stood, in which his actual body now stood, was indeed a control room. He knew the great chambers at the core, though now inert, once generated unimaginable power. And he knew the purpose of the station. The great and terrible reason it was made. It flooded him, the knowledge, the ideas, the impossible truth of it. The great sorrow of loss, the onslaught of centuries of fear and despair. The hope, the bright flicker of anticipation of deliverance. He felt himself being pulled along as if caught in the current of a violent river. Unable to hold on anymore he was swept away with it.

CHAPTER 7

Sara-Jay Schieva sat in the small common compartment of mining shuttle one, looking over the progress of the automated factory being constructed on the larger of the third planet's moons. The nano assemblers were making good progress as there were ample materials for them to scavenge and process into building components. At this rate, the factory would be operational in a few hours. That was good because then they could start building the space hoppers needed to carry exotic ore back to the ship.

The cargo bay on the Philosopher King was large enough for the volume of new exotics typically found in a system. They were usually discovered in small, scattered quantities that had to be meticulously ferreted out. But in this place, they were concentrated everywhere. The crew wouldn't be able to do more than scratch the surface. They would have to employ the technique favored by large mining outfits that exploited whole star systems for large quantities of common ores. Large barges would have to be built with maneuvering thrusters and loaded with the material. These could then be tethered in a train or array and towed by a starship that could incorporate them into its hyperdimensional area of influence. Such a vessel would be far larger than the Philosopher King and have a shadow drive many times more powerful. She'd even heard that such ships could maintain gravity while superluminal. The captain would either have to lease one or partner with another company.

"Buckle up back there, we're ready for lift-off!" Tom Hepner's voice came from the open hatch to the shuttle cockpit. Sara-Jay had agreed to come along and help him survey the third planet. Gus was hoping to get an early start on mapping it out, anticipating the future mining mission that would certainly follow once they got their samples back to the markets of civilization. Gus wanted to have a plan in place and hated wasting time. Sara-Jay could appreciate that. She'd just fastened the buckles on her seat when Ava stuck her head in from the cockpit.

"Are you ready back there?" Ava said. "Tom's ready to go." Ava was the other current occupant of the shuttle. Sara-Jay wasn't quite sure if Tom had invited her specifically or if she'd invited herself. Either way, the two had spent the last several minutes chatting away while she'd busied herself checking on the construction status. The rest of the two teams were staying on the moon to continue the work. A small prefab operations hub had been erected first, along with a tiny crew quarters module. What team members weren't currently bouncing around outside in envirosuits were clustered inside it.

"I'm ready when you guys are," said Sara-Jay, managing a smile.

Ava smiled back, and, still looking at Sara-Jay, called out, "She's ready Tom, we can go now." Ava ducked back into the cockpit, presumably to buckle up herself. The hatch door shut, and Sara-Jay was left to her solitude as she felt the first bout of acceleration as the shuttle lifted off the moon's surface to make its way to the planet below.

The shuttle glided down the gravity well and entered the atmosphere close to the equator on the sunward side. There was no point in putting down in the middle of night. After executing his approach, Tom Hepner landed on a large plateau in a clearing among a collection of jagged rock formations. Once the landing protocols were completed and the engines had cooled down, he and the two women donned their envirosuits and cycled through the airlock.

Sara-Jay always found it unnerving to set foot on alien soil, but especially within an atmosphere. She was mostly used to walking on moons and asteroids beneath the great black void of space, broken only by the silent vigil of the stars. Now she was beneath a bright blue sky with wispy pink clouds, and even through her suit, she could feel the press of a gentle breeze. It was earth-like enough to almost fool her senses into believing that she was back on one of the colony worlds but different enough to still invoke the uncanny valley.

"I'm going to deploy the survey drones and do a fifty-click radial sweep," said Tom. His voice over the intercom pulled her out of her musings. Sara-Jay activated her heads-up display and patched into the shuttle's sensors. She directed them to start an active mineral scan of the plateau. Orbital scans could only do so much, and the shuttle's purpose-built sensor module could provide a detailed report of every element, or suspected new element, up to two thousand meters beneath the surface. Having started the scan, Sara-Jay dismissed the display and resumed studying her surroundings. She noticed that Ava had walked over to one cluster of the rock formations and reached out to touch it with a gloved hand. These particular rocks stood about twenty meters tall and were arranged in a straight line like a wall.

"This is some weird mess," Ava said.

"How do you mean?" asked Tom. He was still working on deploying the drones. Sara-Jay walked over to get a better look at what Ava was talking about.

"I mean, it's just weird," said Ava. "There's all these shapes and designs and then there's this circle here." She pointed to a circle about a hand's breadth wide at eye level on one of the rocks. As Sara-Jay got closer, she could see that what had appeared from a distance to be a rough surface was actually an intricate lattice of geometric shapes covering the whole rock-face. The shapes were blurred here and there, and as she studied them, she noted that they were not etched into the rock, but painted somehow and covered by a thin patina of brown sediment. She rubbed the rockface with her fingers. The sediment fell off readily, and bright colors began to shine through from beneath.

Ava followed her lead, and within a few minutes, the two had uncovered a small section around the circle that contained a kaleidoscope of colored shapes. It was beautiful in its way. Everything had a metallic tint, but the colors ran the full spectrum, from bright reds to soft blue pastels. The circle situated among these shapes was green, and Sara-Jay almost thought she saw it glow a little. She blinked, and the effect was gone.

"Wow," Ava said, sounding almost wistful. "Somebody did that." It was true. This was no natural formation. Sara-Jay glanced around at the other formations. Were they all decorated like this beneath the sediment? Tom walked over, abandoning his drone setup to see what had drawn his two companions to the rocks. Then suddenly, when he had closed about half the distance, he shouted over the com.

"Ava!" Sara-Jay turned back to look at the woman who was now standing dead still, shoulders slumped, staring directly at the green circle. "Ava!" Tom shouted again, this time louder, but she didn't reply. He was almost to her when suddenly the green circle recessed back into the rockface, and the surrounding section began to part from the middle. That brought Tom up short as he and Sara-Jay watched the two sections slide outwards revealing a large oval opening and a chamber beyond. And then Ava screamed.

* * *

The next thing Ander Navarro knew he was lying on the observation bed staring at the ceiling in the Philosopher King's med bay.

"Welcome back," Dr. Ellison said as she stepped over to the bed. Ander blinked, then slowly opened his mouth. It felt dry, and like he hadn't used it for anything in a very long time. He glanced to the side, noticing that both the captain and Jill Thomas were staring down at him.

"Are you okay?" the captain asked.

Ander started to answer, but then paused to take stock of himself. He could feel his legs and arms. That was good. He felt a little bit like he had back in university, when someone spiked the drinks at a party he'd reluctantly gone to. He'd blacked out then and ended up at the medical center. However, other than his throat feeling dry, he thought he was more or less all right.

"Uh, yes sir, I believe I am okay." Ander's voice was raspy, and it took some effort to speak. "How long have I been here?"

"You've been out for a whole day," Jill said.

"Twenty-two standard hours to be exact," the doctor said.

"Do you feel anything strange?"

Ander was about to say again that he was okay, but then he noticed something. There *was* something strange, something at the tip of his awareness. But he wasn't sure what it was. There was some other part to his recent experience that he almost remembered.

"I think I feel well enough," Ander said. And with that, his encounter with the alien came rushing back into his recollection. The impressions, the numbers, the emotions, and a history of what had happened centuries ago. It threatened to overwhelm him again, but he managed to tap it down and by force of will grasped control of his mind. When the moment passed, he looked soberly at the captain. "Captain, we have to talk."

* * *

Thirty minutes later Ander was sitting at the holographic table in the conference room. Captain Spear was there, along with Jill Thomas, the doctor, Maxwell Forrester, and Jax Dyson whose penetrating gaze unnerved Ander. John Terry and Gus Masterson entered a few minutes after everyone else and took their seats. Phil was there too, of course, since the synthetic intelligence was everywhere aboard ship.

"Okay," Ander began after the captain gave him a nod to start. "What I'm going to say is going to sound a little weird. But I believe that I, or at least my mind, was pulled into shadow space when I activated the sphere. I think this is what happened to me earlier too but to a lesser degree. I've already given the captain the highlights, but basically, I think that these spheres are some kind of interface terminals, similar to the helm interfaces we use when controlling the shadow drive and navigating hyperdimensional space." He glanced at the doctor.

"The effects on Ander's brain activity are similar to what we see in someone piloting a starship over an extended faster-than-light trip, but to an even greater degree," she said. "In fact, I'm recommending that Ander be excused from helm duty for the immediate future. I'm concerned that his brain scans look far too similar to those of pilots who burned themselves out back before we established safety guidelines for how long a person can operate a shadow drive. But more to Ander's point, I concur that his brain was engaged with hyperdimensional space, just in a different way than we are familiar with."

"Anyway," Ander said, picking up his story, "while I was in there, I think I made first contact. There was an entity of some sort there, and it talked with me. It showed me a schematic of the station and where there is damage that's preventing the station from fulfilling its purpose."

"Its purpose?" Maxwell said, arching an eyebrow. Jax sat beside him unmoving, his face granite.

"Yes," said Ander. "That's the other thing. I had a lot of information dumped into my head. Impressions, statistics, technical data. I've been trying to feed it all to Phil before I forget any of it. But the gist is this: this is not a naturally exotic-rich star system, as we first thought. This is a graveyard. It's the home of an alien species, a sentient alien species. The rich minerals and exotics are a result of their infrastructure and to some extent the calamity that befell it." Maxwell's eyebrow managed to arc even higher, but he held his peace for the moment. "You see," Ander continued, "there was a star in this sector that went supernova some centuries back, three hundred and twenty-six Earth years to be exact. It sent out a massive radiation wave that blanketed most of this sector of space. And the people here were mostly annihilated by it. The people, the flora and fauna of the worlds, their infrastructure, everything."

"You said *mostly* annihilated," Gus Masterson said.

"Yes, Chief Masterson. I said *mostly* because the people, that is the aliens, had been studying the particular star that went supernova for years and were aware of its impending destruction and what it would mean for their civilization."

"You can just call me Gus," said Gus, "or, Chief works too."

Ander nodded, still not sure how to address the older man.

"Did they evacuate the system?" Maxwell asked.

"Well," Ander said. "That's the thing. In many ways, I get the impression that they had technology beyond our own, but they never developed a way to travel faster than light."

"And even if they had started in the opposite direction into deep space," John Terry said, "they'd never get far enough out at subluminal speeds to escape the blast radius."

"That's right," Phil said. "Based on the information that Ander has given me and comparing it to our own star charts, it appears that the star that went supernova was about five light-years away, in what we now know as the Armada Nebula Cluster. Data is consistent with a massive supernova occurring there within the last five centuries."

"Not to mention the logistics and supply issues of keeping a whole civilization alive on generation ships until they arrived, who knows where, after centuries of travel," Jill said.

"So," Ander continued, "they came up with an alternate solution." He paused for effect. Perhaps it was a bit theatrical, but he wanted to make sure he had their undivided attention. "They somehow pushed themselves into shadow space."

There was another pause. Maxwell looked skeptical. Jax

remained a statue, and Jill Thomas winced. Everyone else looked thoughtful, considering the possibility, except for the doctor whose glance jumped from face to face wanting someone to comment on whether something like that was even possible.

"That would take a *lot* of energy," John Terry said. "And involve some very specific parts of the spectrum."

"So let me see if I know where this is going," said Jill. "These beings are supposed to be in shadow space somehow, and they want us to repair the space station. Is the station somehow connected with them being able to return to normal space? Is that its purpose?"

"Well, yes," said Ander. "The space station was damaged by the energy wave and they were never able to return after the event was over."

"So they've been somehow surviving there for centuries?" asked Spear. "They must be very long-lived. Did they bring food and supplies with them into shadow space somehow?"

"Well," said John, "we're in completely theoretical territory now, but if they did manage to collapse themselves into shadow space, physical three-dimensional processes like metabolism would probably be impossible. I'm still not convinced of any of this, but if this is not just some elaborate charade or miscommunication, then I would imagine it'd be somewhat like being in stasis."

"Doctor, what do you think about all of this?" asked the captain.

"I don't know," she said. "This technology is well outside of anything I'm familiar with. But if we are dealing with truly alien biology, then human considerations may not apply, regardless of how organic material would react to being shoved into hyper dimensions."

"I have a question," said Maxwell. "When you talk about these aliens returning, what do you mean exactly? Are you saying they will all somehow materialize into the station? How many are we talking about?"

"Ten thousand, four hundred, and twenty-four," said Ander. "That's the number that kept being impressed on my mind."

"Will that many fit in the station?" asked Maxwell.

"That is impossible to estimate without knowledge of the aliens' physical dimensions or their life support requirements," said Phil.

"I don't think they're all going to be returning to the station," said Ander. "One of the things I remember is seeing images of beings being translated when the station was initially activated. It's a little fuzzy now, but I remember that some of them were inside what might have been the station, but most appeared to be standing outside, in the open air. I think whatever process they came up with, it was system-wide. I think the return process is supposed to be similar. The ten thousand number is a fraction of how many were originally translated. They impressed upon me that the place where they are now is shrinking somehow and that the remaining ones are at risk."

"That certainly does add a sense of urgency," said Jill.

Jax Dyson, whose expression had heretofore remained blank and unmoving, turned to look at her contemplatively. Spear noticed it and was about to ask the man to share his thoughts when Phil broke in suddenly.

"Captain and officers, I'm receiving an incoming transmission from our mining team on the third planet. It's marked as urgent."

* * *

Ava hit the ground hard enough to knock the wind out of her lungs. She gasped, and her envirosuit upped the oxygen ratio in response to her struggle for air. Tom and Sara-Jay were now standing over her staring down.

"Wha... what in the deep black void just happened!?" she finally managed. The other two helped her to her feet.

"We were just about to ask you the same thing," said Sara-Jay.

"It looks like you opened a door!" said Tom starting to sound a little excited now that Ava seemed to be okay.

"All I know," Ava said, "was that I was looking at that gaudy green circle, and it started to glow. The next thing I know I'm falling on my butt and you two are looking at me like you've just seen a ghost!" She roughly brushed some of the dust off her suit in a last bout of frustration and then joined the other two regarding the open portal.

"You know," said Sara-Jay, "I'm beginning to think that we're not the first people to come here."

"Oh! I think we're the first people," said Tom, sounding very excited. "This is big! This is very big! We need to go inside!"

"We don't know that the door won't shut again, trapping us," said Sara-Jay.

"What are you talking about?" asked Ava.

"First contact," said Tom. "This could be first contact! Or at least the ruins of a long-dead race of beings."

"Ancient aliens?" asked Sara-Jay.

"Aliens?" said Ava, sounding a bit awestruck.

"We need to be sure the door won't shut again before anyone goes in," said Sara-Jay.

Tom looked around, impatience showing on his face through his visor.

"What if we use some of the mining equipment from the

shuttle to keep the door wedged open?" he asked. Sara-Jay thought for a moment. There was no guarantee that the mechanisms in the door wouldn't be strong enough to crush whatever they used. However, it seemed unlikely that a door not exposed to hard vacuum would be built robust enough to bend the shaft of the portable mineral bore.

"The mineral-bore shaft," she said finally. "We can use that."

The three went back to the shuttle and retrieved the shaft, which they carefully placed in the threshold of the portal before going in. The interior was dark, and they each engaged their helmet lights as they looked around. They were in what seemed to be a large central chamber with other round portals leading off to smaller side rooms. Some of these portals were all the way open, some partially closed, and some completely shut. Sara-Jay noticed that the walls near each of the doorways had a green circle like the one outside.

The interior was cluttered by what appeared to be furniture of unusual shape and proportion. Nothing Sara-Jay saw seemed to be suitable for the human physique. Thin pedestals throughout the space sported shiny colored spheres. They too seemed to glow if she let her eye rest on them for a few seconds, like what she'd experienced outside with the green circle. Sara-Jay decided she would be extra careful not to look at any one thing for too long. The last thing she wanted was to accidentally trigger some other mechanism. After they'd looked around a bit, the three gathered again in the center of the room.

"Everything seems to be dead," said Tom. "My suit sensors pick up a very slight electromagnetic field when I get close to the walls, but it's just barely more than the background radiation on this planet."

"It's a little stronger near some of the doors," said Ava. She had made a circuit around the perimeter of the chamber and explored a few of the smaller side rooms that were open.

"I pick up a slight elevation in intensity when I step close to one of these colored spheres," Sara-Jay said, pointing to a bright purple one.

"So, what are we thinking?" asked Ava.

"Aliens for sure!" said Tom.

"Aliens probably," said Sara-Jay. She was a little surprised at her own lack of skepticism, but something about this place spoke to her intuition in a way that was definitely not human.

"That's kind of creepy," said Ava.

"We need to know more," said Sara-Jay.

"Agreed," said Tom. "But I don't think we're going to get much more from this structure right now. It seems to be powered down, aside from the odd door mechanism. I was hoping we'd find something else working inside here, but maybe it's just been too long."

"So, no first contact?" asked Ava.

Tom had been looking up at the chamber's ceiling, but he presently turned to glance back at her and smiled broadly.

"Oh, it's still first contact for us!" he said.

"We should probably determine whether this place is an anomaly or if similar ruins exist elsewhere on the planet," said Sara-Jay.

Tom looked thoughtful.

"You're right," he said. "I need to get the drones in the air. I can program them to specifically look for structures like this one. We'll need to update Gus and the captain."

"Yes," said Sara-Jay. "But I'd like to know more about what we're dealing with before we send a transmission. If this whole planet was the home to a long-dead alien species then this is likely no longer a mining claim, but an archaeological one. Let me help you with that programming. I think we can use the drones' mineral sensors to penetrate the patina and look for patterns similar to the ones on this structure."

"Absolutely," said Tom, and then he nodded at the two of them. "Let's see what's out there."

* * *

"Go ahead," said Spear. The center of the conference table illuminated, and a near-life scale hologram of Sara-Jay Schieva materialized in front of everyone. It was a prerecord message since the Philosopher King was several light minutes away from the main planet and a two-way conversation would be riddled with delay. She began to speak. Her tone was professional, but her eyes betrayed excitement. The captain wasn't sure at first if that excitement was alarm or enthusiasm. As the message played, he decided it was probably a little of both.

"Philosopher King, Chief Masterson, Captain Spear, I wanted to contact you because we've discovered something rather remarkable out here. It appears that the third planet is not the untouched treasure trove of materials that we thought on first inspection. After making several aerial scans using our survey drones and doing some onsite investigation, we believe that this planet was once the home to a civilization of some kind. Everything looks mostly dead, and we estimate, based on the condition of the structures we've seen, that it's probably been centuries since any of it was occupied.

"Nonetheless, as much of the planet as we have been able to observe appears to be covered with ancient abandoned cities connected by a highly ordered network of roadways and infrastructure. We are planning to continue scanning to see if we can map out the entire planet for study. I also recommend that we be on the lookout for other evidence of previous inhabitants elsewhere in the system.

"I have attached to this message the parameters we programmed our drones with to identify artificial structures. The buildings are covered with some kind of markings or script. We've been scanning as much as we can for future analysis." She paused briefly before continuing. "Captain, our team thinks that the origins of these ruins are non-human. I tend to agree with that assessment." She paused again, took a breath, and said, "Schieva out," without further elaboration.

The hologram disappeared, but most eyes were still glued to the empty space it had occupied.

"Well," said Jill Thomas, "that would certainly seem to correspond with what we are learning from the station. I noticed she avoided using the word 'alien.'"

"Should I halt mining operations?" asked Gus.

"No, not yet," said Spear. "Send your crews a message and forward them the scan parameters Ms. Schieva sent us. Just have them be careful and avoid anything that looks artificial or bears those markings."

"So, what are we going to do?" asked Jill.

"I think," said Spear, "we are going to start repairing that space station."

CHAPTER 8

Ander spent the next several hours being debriefed by Phil. Everything he said was recorded, and he could feel it leaving his mind even as he recited it. It was as if in speaking it out loud, he released the knowledge the strange aliens had given him. Phil's recollection, however, was far less ephemeral, and the ship's engineers began translating the information into an understanding of the space station's systems and plans for repairing them.

Some of the damaged systems were relatively easy to repair. Others required a great deal of improvising with results that were temporary at best. The Philosopher King was far from a space dock, but the mining and manufacturing equipment was repurposed for the task.

As for the mining operations, Spear ordered that they continue in locations where there was no evidence of alien structures or artifacts. It was true that the archeological groups would probably complain later that he hadn't suspended them completely, but Spear enterprises had expenses. He was way out on a limb trying to repair the broken space station. His mining claim on the system would supersede any archeological objection as a matter of law, but besides that, he mused, how could he cause any more damage than what the nearby supernova had already done?

Spear was on the bridge, sitting in the captain's chair and looking over some cost projections when John Terry's voice came over the com to announce that the repairs outlined by Ander and Phil were complete.

"I'll be honest with you, skipper," John said, "I have no idea if this thing will bring those aliens back when we flip the switch or just blow itself to kingdom come. I followed the instructions, and some of it made sense to me, like where we repaired power conduits and fried out circuits. But I have no idea how the rest of it is even *supposed* to work. Not even theoretically." He paused and let out a slow breath that Spear could hear over the signal. He was deep somewhere in the station. "But for good or ill, if we're actually going to try this madness, then we are ready over here."

"How far do you think we should position the Philosopher King from the station just in case?" asked Spear.

"I'd feel better if we were at least a hundred thousand clicks," John said. "That might give us time for some evasive maneuvers if parts come flying our way. I can have the sub-light engines fully powered up and ready to move in a hurry."

"Okay, then let's get everyone out of there, and we'll move into position," said Spear.

"Well, we can't get everyone out," said Terry. "Someone will have to stay behind to activate the system."

"Can't we activate it remotely?" asked Spear.

"Well, the controls on these systems are exclusively activated by a hyperdimensional interaction. There's not a solid switch, button, or holopanel in the whole station. Someone has to stay behind, and that someone should probably be a pilot. They're the only ones trained to use an interface similar to this."

"I'm not sure I'm comfortable asking anyone to stay behind when it activates," said Spear.

"You don't have to ask," said Terry. "We have a volunteer."

"Let me guess: Ander," said Spear.

"Got it in one," said Terry. "He's obsessed with this whole thing."

"Thanks, John," said Spear. "Get your teams back to the ship."

"Roger that, skipper," said Terry and cut the connection.

"Phil," said Spear, "Where is Ander Navarro now?"

"Ander is still on the space station," said Phil.

"Let me talk to him. Bring him up on the holoscreen."

In the front of the bridge, the holoscreen came to life, and that section of the bridge was replaced by a holographic re-production of Ander Navarro and his immediate surroundings. Ander started as he was alerted that the connection had been established. He straightened from the spherical console he was standing over. Spear could see a few coveralled engineers milling around behind him just at the edge of the holoscreen's periphery.

"Captain," Ander said in greeting.

"I hear you've volunteered to stay behind," said Spear.

"Yes sir, just to activate the process. It has to be initiated via a direct hyperdimensional interface, like our shadow drive system. Only a trained pilot will be able to activate it correctly, and we can't do it remotely."

"So I am told," said Spear. "You know that we have no idea what will actually happen when this thing powers up."

Ander didn't miss a beat.

"Yes, sir, but John, Phil, and I have gone over the repairs and the systems involved dozens of times, and it all looks to be just like the aliens described it to me." A large figure stepped into the field of view of the holoscreen behind Navarro and loomed over him. "I understand the risks, sir," Ander continued, oblivious to the newcomer. "I am inclined to trust the aliens."

A large hand clapped down on Navarro's shoulder, causing him to jump.

"Which is why I will be the one to activate the station," Jax Dyson's grim voice said as he peered up at Spear from the holoscreen. "With your permission, of course, captain."

Ander looked as though he was about to protest, but the captain spoke first.

"You sense trouble?" asked Spear.

"Most of my career has been spent exploring and recovering artifacts from old derelict ships and stations, and there's always trouble of some sort. No offense to Mr. Navarro, but I feel like there are more notes to this tune than we are hearing."

Ander opened his mouth again to speak, but the captain again cut him off.

"Ander, you are our highest-rated pilot. If this thing goes south, I want you at the helm. Jax, I can't ask you to do this."

"It will be done," said Jax. "This is too big a discovery, too big a temptation. Someone else will do it if I don't. Someone else would have repaired this station eventually. It is too much to leave alone. I will do the inevitable." Then he was silent, just staring.

"Make sure you have a quick evac route to the shuttle, just in case those other notes start playing," said the captain. "And Godspeed."

* * *

The dark void of space that hung between the Philosopher King and the alien space station slowly grew as the King rotated away from the strange monstrosity and ignited its sub-light reaction drive. On the bridge, Spear sat in the command chair watching the forward holoscreen as it maintained a virtual representation of the space station slowly rotating on its axis. Ander was to his left, deftly manipulating the controls and watching his flight data readout. He glanced at the holoscreen every few seconds. The captain noticed this.

"I'm sure Jax has it under control," the captain said. Ander turned briefly to look at him before returning his gaze to his controls.

"I'm sure he does, Captain," he said. "I just wonder what it's going to be like afterward."

"After we make official contact with the first ever discovered alien society?" asked the captain.

"Yes, I mean back when they first invented the shadow drive and we were finally able to leave our solar system, people expected to run into alien life of some sort. But then it didn't happen, and I think everyone just got used to the idea again that we were the only ones. Like God decided one little speck of life in the whole universe was good enough. And now, yet again, we have that all upended." Ander looked like he meant to say more, but no words came.

"Well, it is certainly quite the reversal," said Spear. "But I think the answer is simply that the universe is vast. We're only a few generations removed from the first faster-than-light spaceflight. My great-grandfather was among the first colonists on Alpha Centauri. We've only just begun to explore our little corner of the galaxy. Creation may be teaming with life and beings, like these, beyond our comprehension, but we just haven't reached them yet."

"Maybe so," said Ander, but Spear could tell the answer didn't satisfy him.

$$* * *$$

Jax stood in one of the rooms just off the corridor adjacent to the large hangar where they'd initially gained access to the station. He stared at a purple orb that was designated the activation control for the station's dimensional displacement device. It was tagged as such by the engineering team. In fact, as they identified the controls for various systems, they tagged several of the colored spheres throughout the station. He concentrated. He reached out with his focus and tried to engage the orb. It didn't take long. Jax had been a gifted helmsman in his youth. In that former life, he'd logged more parsecs than most at the helm of a navy shadow drive. Ander, true to his vocation, had treated these strange artifacts like they were navigation interfaces. Jax did the same now. He relaxed and opened his mind to the datastream that now filtered into his perceptions.

An otherworldly sensation washed over him. It was similar to what happened in the little ship in the hangar, but far more intense. Then, almost as if awakening from a dream, Jax found himself standing beside his body as it still gazed upon the orb. He shifted his consciousness and looked around the room knowing that what he was seeing was the upper dimension of the physical room on the station. He knew it was not a true out-of-body experience. He'd had one of those before. This was his mind expanding beyond his normal senses, but unlike the shifting patterns and shapes one saw while piloting, everything was more substantial here.

Jax searched the room, and there they were. Not just one this time as Ander had described but five, here in the room with him. They were like spirits. They were silent, and all stood stark still except one who moved among the other control orbs as if it was checking readouts. Jax felt something stirring—a rift in reality that blurred the lines between the hyperdimensional realm and the normal three dimensions of physical reality. He knew that the process had already been started. His activation of the interface had triggered it. He supposed that had been by design, but he had thought there would be some interaction on his part, perhaps an "are you sure you want to continue?" prompt in his mind.

Jax was suddenly aware of vast numbers of them. Like specters from the hereafter, they floated into existence. The station was drawing them back, he knew. He could understand more and more of its operation by the second as data poured into his brain. He knew what seemed like several minutes was taking place in the blink of an eye in normal time. They were crossing over, coming back from the reality of the exile they had consigned themselves to in hopes of escaping the deadly energy wave from the supernova. Thousands started to materialize on the station, and beyond that, he could sense millions now across the solar system, returning to life, to reality.

He remembered that the number of survivors they had given to Ander was much smaller than what he was seeing now. What had been their homeworld was now a giant glowing light in Jax's mind as he felt an entire civilization transitioning. He briefly wondered what they would be coming back to and the challenges they would face rebuilding their society. He wondered how the centuries spent in shadow space would affect their psyches. Would many of them return sane? And why had they lied to

Ander about how many of them still survived? Jax suspected he knew the answer to that last question. Downplaying their numbers would make them seem less threatening, and claiming they were dying off in their hyperspace refuge might motivate their would-be rescuers to act more quickly—and perhaps rashly.

And then he noticed something else. Lights, specs of radiance where individual aliens had reappeared out in the solar system, between the worlds, followed by what his mind could only recognize as a set of vectors and arcs. Then it dawned on him. Not unlike the navigational plotting done by human pilots, these were thousands of intended courses, ordered and locked into place for small alien ships throughout the solar system. Their sensors hadn't detected any vessels so these must have been dormant, perhaps shielded to survive the energy wave.

But they were alive now and tied into the station's communication system. Jax understood their orders, orders that emanated from the station itself, headings and vectors that all converged at one singular spot in space. The coordinates of the Philosopher King flashed across Jax's mind as well as information about its current heading and speed. And more alarming, he recognized something that resembled a tactical analysis. He couldn't have put it into words. The aliens had very different concepts of language, but he knew. Down in his gut, he knew. The wordless understanding seared into his brain. What's more, he noticed other systems on the station powering up, systems that Ander had made no mention of in his debriefing. Jax had read that debriefing carefully. No, these systems resided in sections of the station that John's engineering team hadn't touched. And he could feel the power collecting in them.

Jax also noticed that three of the spectral forms had materialized completely into the room and were moving toward his still-standing body. They moved in regular space-time now, so from Jax's heightened perspective, they crawled at a snail's pace. But Jax knew the fact that he could perceive their motion at all meant that they were converging on him with speed. They were larger than even *his* frame with bulbous torsos and tentacles where legs and arms should be. They also seemed to be wearing some type of fabric for clothing. The overall impression Jax got was that of tall, erect octopuses but with several eyes like a spider circling their entire heads. Each eye was a different color and corresponded to the various colors of the orbs they'd seen on the station.

"Well," thought Jax, "this is why I am here, and not the kid." Ander had been engaged with the orb until it released him. It was now programmed to hold the human user until he could be apprehended by these three aliens charging him. Jax could even get a hint that the alien that had been moving among the orbs had just entered that command. But Jax didn't need permission to be released. In his training for salvaging derelict starships, he'd been taught how to pull his mind forcibly out of a malfunctioning shadow drive interface. It was an essential skill for evaluating and testing old shadow drives. He used it now.

With a psychic snap, Jax was back in his body. With a wet slap of hard knuckles on alien flesh, he turned the nearest attacker's trajectory aside into a stand of orb controls. As tentacles from the second alien latched onto his arm, Jax used his free hand to retrieve a collapsible titanium quarterstaff from his pocket. He deployed it and poked out several of the second alien's eyes before bringing it across the third alien's head so hard it flattened one side. The tentacles on his arm released as the second creature recoiled, grabbing at its now-useless eyes. The first alien started to recover, but Jax was already out the door racing to the hangar where his shuttle waited.

CHAPTER 9

On the bridge of the Philosopher King, Ander stood over Jill Thomas's shoulder as they both watched data pour across the main sensor terminal. Truth be told, Jill felt more than a little crowded with Ander there given the economy of space at the sensor station. But none of the other stations could render as complete of an overview of the information, and his enthusiasm was palpable. She wasn't about to deny him the opportunity to watch the information come in live, especially since his obvious disappointment at not being the one to "throw the switch" to activate the station. The readings coming in were off the charts, and Jill began to understand the magnitude of raw power that must have been used to transition the aliens to their hyperdimensional sanctuary.

That power flowed back into normal three-dimensional space, and the entire star system was awash in it. Jill saw identifiable singular bursts popping up on sensors all across the system with most of them concentrated on the main planet where the mining crew had discovered the ruins. First thousands, then millions, then billions, and she realized that these were individual aliens being returned to normal space.

"It's amazing," she said, but Ander was too transfixed by the readouts to respond at first.

"So, it's working?" asked Spear, swiveling in his command chair to meet her eyes.

"Yes," Jill said. "We're seeing them pop back into normal space all across the solar system, by the billions."

"Billions?" asked Spear. He looked at Ander. "Isn't that a bit more than what we were expecting?"

Ander shrugged.

"I don't know sir," he said. "Maybe I misunderstood."

"Also," continued Spear, looking back at Jill, "the solar system and all of the objects in it have to be in radically different locations than they were centuries ago, so I assume that the station can't be just dropping them back to where they were when this started." It was Jill's turn to look at Ander.

"I don't know," Ander said. "I got the impression that this was a meticulously planned escape, but even with the data they dumped into my brain, most of the details were omitted."

Phil chimed in. "It's possible that the station is using active sensor tracking and an algorithm to return individuals to locations close to the relative positions they were taken from on the respective planets and installations."

"Let's hope that those sensors can tell if the destinations are even habitable anymore. I don't want to think about rescuing people after all this time only to have them materialize somewhere where there's no longer any breathable air," said Jill.

"I think we have done all we can do," said Spear. "As they told Ander, they couldn't stay in shadow space indefinitely. I think we just have to trust that the aliens can handle their part."

Just then the com system activated, and Jax Dyson's voice came over laced with uncharacteristic alarm. It sounded as if he were running.

"Captain, they want the ship. You have to move now, or they'll have us!" His words hung ominously for a heartbeat, and then Phil's voice came back over the speakers.

"I've reevaluated the movements of several objects in the solar system based on Mr. Dyson's assertion, and I can confirm that it appears that several small vessels are maneuvering to intercept us. Also, I am detecting power surges in sections of the space station that were undocumented in the schematics that our engineering teams were given."

"Ander, to the helm!" shouted Spear. "Bridge to Forrester, get to the defense module now, we have potential hostiles. Jax, get to your shuttle. We'll grab you on the go."

"I'm almost to the hangar," said Jax.

"Why would they do this?" Jill wondered out loud. "We were helping them!"

Ander didn't say anything. He was dumbstruck as he reached the helm. That didn't stop him, however, from immediately throwing the ship into evasive maneuvers as he powered up the shadow drive.

"It's the shadow drive," said Spear. "For all their sophistication, they never developed a faster-than-light mode of travel and were trapped here when disaster struck. They want to ensure that it never happens again."

* * *

Jax dashed through the large alien corridor, his long legs propelling him toward the airlock that the engineers had installed in the hanger bay. So far, he had encountered no more resistance since he'd left the control room, but he knew that could change any second. Perspiration dripped from his nose as he grabbed a space suit and helmet from one of the hooks, also installed by the engineers, and quickly sealed up and pressurized. The suits were made to slip on quickly in case of an emergency loss of atmosphere, but as the helmet clicked into place, he caught sight of something emerging from around the curve of the corridor behind him.

It wasn't one of the aliens. Instead, it was a large robot with tentacle arms protruding from a spherical white body. It also appeared to be covered with electronic eyes pointing in all directions. It was so large it occupied the diameter of the corridor. So this was why the hall was so big, Jax briefly thought before retreating into the airlock. He triggered the emergency override once inside so he wouldn't have to wait for the air to cycle. A burst of atmosphere exited with him into the hangar bay.

Once there, he saw two more of the behemoth robots standing beside his shuttle. They turned as if to notice him. He had kept his quarterstaff on the outside of the space suit in case he needed to use it, but he knew it would be ineffective against these machines as they approached him. Meanwhile, the airlock behind him creaked as the robot from the corridor pushed its way through. His escape was cut off. He was trapped. Then, a crazy thought occurred to him, an idea of how he might yet get off of this malicious space station. It wouldn't be easy, and in truth, he thought it was certain to fail as he turned and dashed off, toward the small alien ship he'd crashed earlier.

* * *

Maxwell Forrester had been in the small operations nook that adjoined the engineering bay, monitoring all of the sensor data coming from the space station and the system at large. The operations nook could function as a backup bridge in an emergency and was the perfect place for him to stay on top of the situation as they activated the station without being in anyone's way up on the bridge. John Terry had been standing with him watching the panorama of screens when the captain's voice resonated over the com. Maxwell had noticed the movements of the small craft throughout the system and was just about to call the bridge himself, seeing too what appeared to be intercept paths. He and John were both in motion now, John running to strap down at the main engineering station, and Maxwell racing through the hatch and down the corridor to the lift that would take him to the outer deck, where the defense module was located.

The Philosopher King's defense module was an upgrade that Joshua Spear opted for when he purchased the ship. It took two weeks to install and was expensive, but the captain thought it a prudent investment for a ship that would spend so much of its time on the outer fringe of known space. It was a circular affair, about fifteen meters in diameter that plugged into an expansion bay on the forward "top" of the ship. It encompassed the entirety of the King's defensive capabilities with a rotating rail gun, twelve deployable point defense drones armed with particle beams, and three larger intercept drones that carried small antimatter warheads designed to be used offensively like missiles. Maxwell hoped that he wouldn't have to employ those. This gave the King more tactical capability than most non-military vessels, but as he strapped into the chair and watched the multitude of potential bogies light up the sensor display, it felt woefully insufficient.

Maxwell powered up the system and immediately launched the point defense drones. Hatches around the perimeter of the module opened and the small drones launched, falling into preprogrammed orbits around the hull of the Philosopher King, their small thrusters lighting off as they struggled to keep up with the evasive maneuvers Ander was taking the ship through. They swarmed around the ship like worker bees protecting their queen. The railgun deployed next from its own hatch and the whole module rotated with it as Maxwell began tracking potential targets.

A flash of bright light made Maxwell flinch as it registered on his screens fed by optical telescopes. There were no windows in the defense module. It took three successive flashes before he realized that the drones were knocking out incoming projectiles. If he'd been just a few seconds later getting them deployed, the hull would likely have holes in it now. He tracked until he found the bogie responsible. It was a small craft no bigger than a shuttle that had launched from the space station. It had four wingmates that were also almost in range. Thankfully, most of the craft in the system now streaking toward them at breakneck speed were coming from farther away, and it would be a while before they became threats. He keyed the com.

"Captain, we have confirmed incoming fire," Maxwell said. "Defense systems are mitigating. I officially request authorization to engage in active defensive activities." By interstellar shipping law, only the captain, or acting captain, if the former were incapacitated, could authorize the use of offensive weapons. The rail gun and the intercept drones would not fire or deploy without logged authorization from the ship's commander.

"Understood Maxwell, let the log show that I, Joshua Spear,

lawful commander of the Philosopher King authorize the use of offensive weaponry at the date and time stamp of this communication."

And with that Maxwell honed in on the closest of the attacking craft.

* * *

Jax Dyson sprinted across the hangar bay and dove into the still-open hatch on the small alien ship. He pulled it shut behind him and found the strange orb control that had captivated his attention a few days before. He hadn't known what he was doing then. And truthfully, he still didn't know what he was doing now. But he understood the experience better after interacting with the station controls. That had instilled in him a sense of familiarity that was reminiscent of how he interacted with a shadow drive. His big gamble—in fact, his only hope—was that the system would respond and provide the relevant piloting information to his mind. He also hoped that the aliens didn't have some remote way to shut down the vessel or none of this would matter.

He focused on the orb, reaching out with his mind and engaging it like he had the control that activated the station. Just at that moment, time slowed to a crawl again, and he could see himself from the outside as his body stood rigid and transfixed. At first, nothing else happened, but as he looked around the cockpit, at each component, information streamed into his awareness. It wasn't language as he knew it, but an understanding. It was as if everything in the cockpit had its own context menu, and he only had to focus on it for it to begin spewing information into his head. He focused his awareness rather than his physical eyes since they were frozen in place like the rest of his body. Lots of information, but no real understanding of how to power up the ship, much less pilot it. He hoped that it *could* be powered up. The engineers had initially thought the vessel was devoid of energy and that this was why it had drained his envirosuit. But they'd also thought the station was dead and powerless. It wasn't, just in need of repair. Jax's intuition—or maybe it was latent knowledge passed to him by his interface with the station—told him that this little vessel wasn't dead either if only he could wake it up.

Finally, Jax looked straight at the forward bulkhead of the ship where one might expect to find a window or a holoscreen, though neither were present. He focused his attention on that one blank spot, and then suddenly, as if waking from a dream, his frozen body and the entire interior of the ship disappeared and he was standing in the hangar bay once more. Or rather, *standing* was not the right word. He no longer had any sense of his legs, feet, or the rest of his body. In his periphery, Jax noticed the robots that had been standing over his transport shuttle earlier were approaching and had almost reached him from across the hangar bay. A third robot that he assumed to be the one from the corridor trailed them. They moved slowly, but Jax didn't know if it was because they were incapable of rapid movement or if they just knew that he had nowhere to go and were in no hurry.

After a brief delay, his view shifted to focus on them. It also seemed he was looking down at them as if he was hovering somehow. Jax felt this sudden shift might have bothered his stomach if he still had any awareness of it. Curiously, the robots stopped moving and now only peered up at him. He wanted to back away, and his view did drift backward as he thought of it. The robots remained motionless. He could now also see shrouded figures climbing into the other alien ships docked at the far end of the hangar. The ships began to levitate and transverse the length of the hanger toward the far wall, which parted before them.

It finally dawned on Jax what was happening. The thought made him feel both foolish for not understanding before and in awe at the wonder of it. He now saw from the perspective of the alien ship. He was hovering over the hangar bay floor, staring down at his pursuers who were at a loss for how to handle the situation. No doubt his body was still standing frozen in the cockpit while his mind moved the ship by mere will. He knew his body wasn't strapped into a seat. He hadn't even seen any seats or seat belts in the vessel, so he decided he had no choice but to hope that the aliens' technology would somehow protect his body from the g-forces of space flight. It was a desperate hope, but one based on an educated guess. Jax turned his focus to the still-opening hangar bay door and, through sheer force of will, raced his purloined craft after the other alien ships into the cold dark embrace of space.

* * *

Normally, Ander enjoyed a piloting challenge. He prided himself on his piloting skills and had left his cushy spaceliner gig in large part because he'd felt underutilized in that role. He even took a slight pay cut to join the Philosopher King. About right now, however, he was beginning to question his decision as he rolled the ship through turn after turn, trying to make its trajectory and course harder to predict by the alien fighters. He thought of them as fighters. They may not be. They may be just service shuttles with some armaments. But they were shooting something at them, and so, as far as Ander was concerned, they were fighters. Another flash of light lit up the holoscreen as one of the point defense drones atomized an incoming projectile. Ander paid it no mind.

The entire crew was strapped down, and loose objects had been secured. But Ander hoped those prone to motion sickness had thought to grab some meds, because as he watched alien craft stream in from every corner of the system, he knew things were about to get dicey. He heard the captain behind him try and fail for the third time to raise Jax Dyson on the coms. They had remained close to the station while they fended off the few ships that had launched from there in hopes of recovering Jax's shuttle, but they had not seen the shuttle or heard from Jax again since his initial warning. Ander knew so far they had been lucky, because the aliens were in some disarray as the transference pulled them back into normal space. That would change, though, as time progressed. Ander knew they had a very limited window to escape, or all of the fancy piloting tricks in the galaxy wouldn't save them. Then Ander heard the order he was grimly anticipating come from the captain.

"Ander, we can't wait anymore for Jax," he said. "Another five ships have launched from the station, from the hangar we were using, where Jax's shuttle was parked. We can't wait for those ships to catch us. Alter course to rendezvous with our mining teams. I've sent them an evac order. We have to get our people out of there."

Ander felt a deep weight settle into his stomach as he turned the ship about. He knew he'd gotten Jax killed. It was as simple as that. He'd been so focused on helping the aliens and so ecstatic at their very existence that the danger had seemed faint and far away. Now it was up close and personal. Ander set his jaw and determined he would not let anyone else die because of his naivete. The four remaining alien craft turned to make another pass. Four, because Maxwell Forrester had managed to nail one of them with the railgun on the last pass. The small triangular ship had turned to space dust instantly when the line of inert projectiles impacted it at near-light speed. The apparent fragility and lack of countermeasures seemed to confirm that these were not purpose-built military craft.

Ander turned the ship to face the oncoming enemy, pointing the rear of the vessel outward toward the planet their mining teams had been working at. This gave Maxwell a clear field for fire. The defense drones accordingly moved just forward of the ship placing themselves between the Philosopher King and any incoming fire. Then Ander rotated the twin, massive sub-light reaction engines that hung off either side of the ship, port and starboard, until they faced full-on forward. He then began opening up their fuel lines further. The engines flared bright, and the entire bridge crew was pushed forward into their safety harnesses as the ship raced backward toward their mining operations. Ander accelerated at the maximum rate the safety protocols allowed. The ship could handle far more acceleration, but there was only so much its occupants could take before blacking out. Hydraulic compensators on the engine frames helped take the bite out of the initial change in direction, but their utility was limited now. The point defense drones had no such limitations and adjusted easily to the new vector, however. One of them flared and disappeared as an enemy projectile caught it as it maneuvered.

* * *

Spear winced. The drones were expensive, and they were the only thing standing between them and certain destruction.

And so, the chase began. The closest of the enemy ships never really separated as they seemed to have no problem accelerating at inhuman rates. Spear had hoped that their maneuverability would be bound by similar constraints as the King, but either the alien's biology was extremely resilient to g-forces or they had some technology that shielded their crews from the effects. It was also possible that they were remotely controlled, but then he would have expected to see everything launch at once. As it was, the craft coming from the station had appeared sporadically and in small numbers here and there. That implied they were launching as pilots became available.

"Phil," Spear said, keeping his eyes glued to the holoscreen at the front of the bridge. "What does the chatter look like in the system right now?"

"Sensors are not detecting significant levels of conventional broadcast activity. There is a massive amount of hyperdimensional activity as the aliens are still transitioning into normal space."

Jill looked over at Spear.

"What are you thinking?" she asked him.

"I'm trying to find a reason for optimism," he replied cryptically.

"Optimism?" She raised an eyebrow.

"Yes Jill," he said. "We should be toast already, but the alien's response has been sporadic so far. I think their equipment is even more damaged and deteriorated than they thought. We don't really know how well they could observe normal space from their sanctuary. What we're seeing here is not a carefully laid trap, but a desperate gamble." Just then, a violent tremor surged through the ship. The lights dimmed for a second, and the holoscreen froze briefly.

"Damage?" shouted the captain. "Are we hit?'

"No sir," said Phil. "An alien projectile was detonated less than one hundred meters to starboard. Three additional defense drones are no longer maneuvering with us. The defense module AI is attempting to reboot them."

Maxwell's voice came over the com next. "Sorry about that, Captain. These things are rather determined."

"Just don't let them scratch the paint job," Spear said. "And I'll make sure you get a little extra in your bonus this year." He looked back over at Jill.

"Still thinking of optimism?" she asked. Her face wore burgeoning panic now.

He didn't answer her this time. He just stared at the holoscreen as the alien craft came in for another pass.

CHAPTER 10

The operations hub the mining crew had set up on the largest moon of the third planet was controlled chaos as Sara-Jay Schieva ran through her checklist. Crews had been recalled from the asteroid belt once the time had come to reactivate the station, but they still had several tons of mined exotics to finish securing for transport. The remaining material-processing equipment and crew habitats on the moon also had to be broken down now that the system's natives were returning home. Many of the team had already donned envirosuits, and the ops hub where Sara-Jay sat was one of just a few structures still maintaining atmosphere. Not much had happened on the moon itself. Here, no structures had survived the centuries of exile and no aliens materialized.

The surface of the planet was a different matter. Tom Hepner had a feed setup from his shuttle, which showed a constant stream of shimmering arrivals. After the three of them returned from the surface and they had received details about the plan to try to retrieve the aliens from shadow space, he insisted on returning to observe the process. He said someone should be down there to welcome them back. Personally though, Sara-Jay thought he just wanted to get his name in the history books.

She watched the aliens through the feed. They seemed mostly confused and disoriented. The ruins of their cities, which they had initially mistaken for natural landforms due to the amount of degradation, would be a far cry from what they'd left and what they'd expected to return to. She wondered how these former metropolis-dwellers would adapt to the post-apocalyptic wilderness they now found themselves in. Would any of them have the basic survival skills necessary to live until they could rebuild? Had they brought back these people—and that's the way she thought of them, tentacles or no—only so that they could starve en masse?

Sara-Jay was thinking about the logistics of a massive human-itarian mission when she noticed three aliens emerge from the crowd and approach the shuttle where the camera was mounted. These three didn't seem to be disoriented like the rest. They also seemed to be uniformly attired and each carrying something in one tentacle arm. *These must be some sort of officials*, she thought.

She saw Tom step forward to meet them as if he'd been waiting for them. As he raised his hand in greeting, one of the threesome pointed the object it was carrying at him and there was a brief flash. She recoiled as Tom's body collapsed and the alien rushed forward, catching him. They raced toward the shuttle, the one carrying Tom's limp form with it. The camera feed went dark. The com system barked to life.

"This is Captain Spear to all mining crews. Prepare for emergency evacuation immediately. The aliens have become hostile. We are en route to pick you up. I need everybody aboard the shuttles and in high orbit when we arrive. You may be docking under fire. I repeat, prepare for emergency evacuation. Abandon any mining equipment or materials not already loaded into shuttles or containers. Avoid all contact with the aliens. I repeat, avoid all contact with the aliens."

The message was jarring and underscored what she'd just seen on the screen. She knew also the captain must have sent it minutes earlier, but the limits of lightspeed had prevented it from arriving in time to warn Tom. Sara-jay felt a heavy weight settle into her stomach as she grabbed her envirosuit and raced to the airlock.

* * *

Jax Dyson was gaining more and more control over his craft with each passing millisecond. The concentrated awareness that the alien interface provided made subjective time stretch out. He mentally probed the responses of the craft and fine-tuned his control. It struck him, not for the first time, how odd it was that machines constructed by beings so alien could interface so neatly with human consciousness. This had been apparent from Ander's interactions and the data dump that he had received, but it seemed improbable. Someone who was a ponderer of the metaphysical—and Jax was a man who spent much of his quiet time doing just that—might speculate that there was a common design or interface to the way intelligent beings conceptualized the universe, even if the underlying wetware varied considerably.

Jax had managed to tuck his craft into a tight formation with the other alien vessels he left the hangar with. He assumed they were unaware that their erstwhile wingman was not one of their kin. Ahead, his awareness focused on the Philosopher King and the martial diorama that lay barely in motion before his enhanced awareness. Everything was in stark relief and incredibly detailed, a testament to the alien sensors. The King's engines had rotated forward, and the ship was backpedaling at increasing velocity with streams of depleted uranium pellets emanating from the lone railgun on the defense module. The ship was both retreating and facing its enemies. These enemies were another wing of alien vessels that had launched ahead of his wing. He saw the point-defense drones performing their desperate dance as they tried to stay in position between the King and her attackers and intercept the incoming projectiles with their short-range beams.

It was a busy scene, a desperate one, and all in slow motion to Jax. He watched a drone explode and then an alien craft splinter under the railgun's withering fire. The King was holding her own, but barely, and as ammunition ran low and more drones went down, it would eventually succumb. Alien reinforcements would only hasten that.

Hmmm, Jax thought. Would it be hoping too much that he might be able to access his own ship's weapons? As soon as he thought about it, his whole awareness seemed to sharpen even further and take on what seemed like a ruddy glow. Something akin to crosshairs began to appear over any ship or object he focused on, and he was suddenly aware he had a complement of forty-five somethings that were available for his use. He said a silent prayer of thanks and concentrated on the alien ship just ahead of him as they came into range of the King.

* * *

Maxwell carefully picked his targets and directed the defense module's AI to make the most of their limited firepower. The AI directed the actual targeting of the railgun, attempting to intersect the flight paths of the alien craft. They maneuvered at significant fractions of the speed of light as they chased the King, which itself was starting to pull some serious acceleration. The gravity alert came on as the ship's drive pumped its inertia into shadow space at a rate that prevented it from simultaneously maintaining the artificial gravity well. Maxwell hardly gave it notice.

He was having a difficult time holding the attackers at bay. They made themselves increasingly hard for the AI to hit while beginning to unload more and more of their missiles at the King. Another defense drone flashed to vapor as it moved into the path of a missile that had survived the drones' point-defense beams. It was a rational, but costly, sacrifice for the AI to make. As another wing joined the aliens, Maxwell felt growing certainty in the pit of his stomach that he was fighting a losing battle.

And then, one of the alien ships did something odd. It fired upon one of its fellows. The other ship never saw the attack from behind coming and took the barrage in full, vaporizing in a briefly brilliant display. Maxwell kept the AI focused on the other ships as he watched it line up and fire again, destroying a second alien craft. He then tagged it as friendly. Could the aliens be divided in their purpose? Were some of them opposed to attacking the Philosopher King and its crew? After the second ship was destroyed, the defector's wingmates caught on and broke formation to target him. The defector, in turn, bobbed and weaved in patterns that looked all too familiar to an old star navy officer like Maxwell.

"Phil!" Maxwell called out.

"I'm here, Mr. Forrester," the synthetic intelligence replied.

"I need a favor. Can we open a radio channel to the alien craft I've designated as a friendly?"

"I don't have an interface spec for encrypted radio connections to the alien ships," Phil said. "Do you want to wide broadcast an open message?"

"No, they've probably pulled enough info out of Ander's brain to understand our language. I don't want them listening in. Can you blink our running lights?"

"I can certainly do that. To what end?"

"I'm going to encode a series of blinks of various duration that represent a message in an old navy code. If who I think is on that friendly alien craft, he'll understand it."

* * *

Jax ran his new ship through a series of evasive maneuvers. Former training kicked in and seamlessly integrated with the alien control scheme. This prevented him from taking any more open shots at the alien ships, but it drew most of their fire from the King, which for its part was still hammering them with the railgun. Jax hoped it would be enough. The odd thing was that in his hyper-perceptual state, it was easier to dodge and plan his course. The abundance of subjective time let him consider his moves and check for mistakes. It was more like playing a game of chess than what he'd become accustomed to back in evasive piloting training. It also gave him time to notice that the King's running lights were starting to blink.

At first, he thought they'd been hit and damaged, but slowly a familiar pattern emerged. Jax wasn't used to reading it this slowly. In his current state, each flash of the lights seemed to drag on for minutes, but the meaning was plain enough. The message said: "Jax come alongside. Execute rear guard pattern epsilon chi. I will cover you." If Jax were still in his body, he might have chuckled. Maxwell Forrester was nothing if not quick on the uptake. He searched the alien control scheme for something controlling his ship's own exterior lights and found it readily. He blinked back a message of acknowledgment: "Copy that, King."

* * *

The mining shuttles got in formation and orbited the moon of the third planet. They were in a rough ring with the center occupied by two cargo containers. The self-propelled containers carried the material they'd managed to extract before finding out that the former inhabitants of the system would be returning, and before things went sideways. Sara-Jay had wondered about what they'd collected. It paled in comparison with what they would have collected from this system if the aliens had truly been long extinct. But the small haul still contained enough exotic material to ensure the Philosopher King was well-funded for years to come. They'd not excavated anything that looked like it was built by the previous inhabitants, not wanting to disturb any archeological sites, but she still wondered if it wasn't theft to take the small amount they'd gathered. That was probably something for the captain to decide.

Right now, however, she wasn't thinking of any of that. As Sara-Jay sat strapped into the co-pilot's seat on mining shuttle two, she watched the zoomed-in view of Tom Hepner's shuttle as it climbed from the planet's surface. It was on course to rendezvous with them at the moon. She figured Tom was probably still alive since the shuttle was flying, and she doubted the aliens would've been able to pull that off so quickly. But then what did *she* know about what they were capable of? Even still, they had dragged him with them into the shuttle rather than leaving him behind. That implied they needed his help.

"What do you think?" asked Ava Turner from the pilot's seat. Sara-Jay looked over at her, struck by the deep concern on the other woman's face. They were all concerned, all scared, but somehow it seemed out of place on Ava. Her guard was down now, and Sara-Jay got the impression she was seeing her for the first time.

"I don't know," Sara-Jay said. "These shuttles don't have any weapons so we can't do anything to them, and they can't do anything to us unless they decide to go for a collision. But that wouldn't make any sense. That wouldn't gain them anything."

"Jared says they're after the shadow drive," Ava said. Jared was one of the engineers on the Philosopher King that Sara-Jay had noticed giving Ava a lot of attention. She wasn't sure that the interest was reciprocated, but he must have been sending her messages while they were evacuating.

"Oh?"

"Yes, the captain thinks they want it because they never invented it and couldn't escape when the shock wave from the supernova came."

"That would make sense," said Sara-Jay. "It might also explain why they were being so aggressive about it. Fear is a powerful motivator. Still, they might have just asked."

"Yeah, I guess being trapped inside a shadow-space bubble for centuries didn't help their paranoia any," said Ava.

"In any case, I don't think we have anything to worry about from that shuttle just yet," said Sara-Jay. Ava looked surprised at that. "I think they hope to join us here in formation and dock with the King. Then they'll try to get to the shadow drive once they're aboard."

"They want to board us?" Ava said, sounding shocked. "Isn't

that a little desperate?"

"I think they are that desperate," Sara-Jay said. Just then the com system came to life, and Tom's voice came over sounding a bit strained.

"Miner one to miner two. Sorry for the delay, I am en route to join the formation." A wave of relief washed over Sara-Jay. He was still alive. She noticed Ava relax; however, her face still wore an uncharacteristically worried expression. "I hope you don't mind us crashing the party," he continued before the connection closed abruptly.

"That was an odd turn of phrase," said Ava.

"He's trying to hint that he has uninvited guests. He doesn't know that we saw what happened, and he's trying to subtly tell us," said Sara-Jay.

"They're probably standing right over him in the cockpit," said Ava.

"I'm going alert the King," said Sara-Jay. "Let them know we'll be bringing company along."

* * *

The large twin sub-light engines of the Philosopher King rotated again, this time facing stern, and began bleeding off the velocity of the ship as it raced backward toward the rendezvous at the third planet's moon. Ander dumped as much of the inertia as he could into shadow space, but he still found himself slammed into the back of his seat as they decelerated. He heard Jill yelp, and the captain exhale. He knew all over the ship crew members were experiencing the same thing, strapped down in their seats. He felt twice—no, scratch that—three times, at least, his normal weight. The ship decelerated, however, and he could see on the forward holoscreen a representation of the mining shuttles and their cargo. They were already breaking formation and making a beeline for the Philosopher King's massive cargo bay doors, which were already opening.

The attacking alien ships fell back and held their distance once the friendly alien ship had taken up formation with the King. Apparently, and miraculously, Jax Dyson was on that ship. The alien ships retreated just out of range, but reinforcements approached from all over the solar system. Ander knew that once they arrived, the attack would resume in force.

"Bridge to Forrester," said Spear.

"Forrester here." came the reply.

"Maxwell, this is going to be close. Tell Jax to fall in with the cargo shuttles. We'll use our cargo crane to grab his ship and secure it. Tell him and the cargo crew to stay put, though, and prepare for heavy acceleration. We won't have time to transfer anyone until we're clear. Also, go ahead and deploy the interceptor drones. Have them stick close to us for now but configure them for detonation and be prepared to feed them to the aliens on my order."

"Aye, aye skipper," said Maxwell.

Spear closed the connection and opened another.

"Gus, how's our pickup coming along?" he asked.

"Bay doors fully open, Captain," came the reply. "Shuttle docking clamps are open, and the main crane is ready to grab and stow the payload."

"Good," said Spear. "Stow it quickly because I need you to use it to grab and hold the alien ship that Jax Dyson is piloting. He'll be following the shuttles into the bay. Can you do that?"

"Shouldn't be a problem, Captain," Gus said. "I'm just a little worried about the velocity we're doing this at. I mean, the equipment is supposed to handle it, but there's no margin for error. One little mistake at these speeds, and we could have a collision that none of us will live to regret."

Spear took a long breath. "I know, Gus, but I know you and your team are the best in the business. If anyone can pull this off, you can. You have my complete confidence."

Another pause.

"Thank you, boss," said Gus. "I'll pass your words along to my team."

The connection closed, and Spear exchanged a glance backward with Jill before turning forward again to look at Ander.

"Mr. Navarro," he said. "It's show time!"

* * *

The Philosopher King's twin sub-light engines flared again, brighter than before, trimming off the last few crucial kilometers per second needed for the mining shuttles to make it into the cargo bay. They came in single file led by mining shuttle two, matching velocity and rotating to align with their respective docking clamps. Ava gave one last tiny burn to the thrusters to orient before the clamps slammed home with a thud. Now relatively motionless, secured to the inner hull of the bay, Sara-Jay watched out the cockpit window as the other shuttles each in turn filed in and locked down. They did so near perfectly, and Sara-Jay heard Ava let out a breath when the last one was secured. Next came the two cargo containers flaring their own thrusters. They rose up into the bay and the massive overhead claw sped down the track and grabbed them one by one. The cargo containers' thrusters disengaged as Gus used the claw to move them each to the cargo clamps at the front of the bay.

Sara-Jay peered over at miner one, which had docked without incident with the rest of the shuttles. Just knowing it contained aliens with malicious intent made the normally bland lines of the shuttle seem malevolent. Then finally came the alien ship. They'd been notified that it would be coming aboard and that somehow Jax Dyson was piloting it. She promised herself that after this was all over, she'd have to ask him how he'd managed to pilot one of their ships. From what she'd heard about him though, she figured he'd only spare her the minimum words necessary if he decided to speak of it at all. Sara-Jay wondered if Joe would have any better luck getting details out of him since he was a fellow pilot. Gus, having secured the cargo, now moved the claw back and used it to expertly grab hold of and secure the strange craft. The giant bay doors in the belly of the ship were now closing but were only about halfway shut when she was unceremoniously slammed back into her seat and the Philosopher King began its escape run.

* * *

The alien ships were coming now. They'd started before the cargo shuttles had even made it in. They were joined by reinforcements that had been inbound almost since the station had come to life. They were almost within range. Ander flipped the ship while maintaining direction and velocity so that the Philosopher King was now facing "forward" again and away from its pursuers. This was necessary to use the shadow drive as it, unlike the sub-light engines, was not designed to propel the ship in reverse. Ander then began pulling the ship upward from the ecliptic of the solar system in a graceful arc as he poured on yet more acceleration. The sub-light engines labored and burned through fuel at an alarming rate. The shadow drive was alleviating some of the g-forces by bleeding off physical inertia into higher dimensions. But it had hit its limit, and Ander now found it difficult to breathe.

"Warning," came Phil's voice. "We are approaching the maximum safety threshold for acceleration. Automatic engine shutdown is imminent."

"This is Captain Joshua Spear," said the captain in a strained voice. "I hereby order that automatic safety threshold considerations be disabled until further notice: authorization code beta alpha Spear three three twenty-nine."

"Code accepted and so-ordered," replied Phil.

"What does it look like, Ander?" Spear asked.

Ander was plugged into the drive interface, his natural perception amplified so that he could see the eddies and currents of shadow space. They were still far too close to the gravity wells of the star and planets to engage and go superluminal. Ander could also see the alien vessels gaining on them. How they were able to take that much acceleration without liquefying their pilots was a mystery to him, but they gained nonetheless.

Ander watched the edges of the gravitational influence of the system fluctuate at the edge. He needed an ebb in the tide, a place where the effect on shadow space would recede for just a moment. Where would such a gap open up? Where would one be that they could get to in time? His mind began to see a pattern emerge. He could almost predict, and then he saw it. There was a spot relatively close, a few million kilometers away where the gravity forces pulled back every thirty seconds or so.

Ander glanced at his chronometer and timed it exactly. It was every twenty-seven seconds, and it lasted for about four seconds before the wave pushed out again. There it was, the gap he needed. It was nearer by at least ten million kilometers than any other opening. He course-corrected slightly and adjusted the acceleration so that they would be exactly where they needed to be when they could activate the shadow drive.

The slight change in course and acceleration, however, allowed the pursuing alien ships to gain a little more. They took the opportunity to launch a barrage of their missiles. In the tactical module, Maxwell saw it on his display and gaped. There were a lot. Too many for the point defense drones to ever take out. The drones had managed to hang with them so far, though they were dangerously low on fuel. He knew too that if the aliens managed to land even one hit, it might disable the ship, and they'd never escape. He said a silent prayer and started prioritizing targets. On the bridge, Spear saw it too.

"Ander," Spear said, "do we have an escape hatch?"

"Yes," said Ander, clearly distracted with his work. "We're on our way, but I need a couple of more minutes to get us there."

"Maxwell, it's time to use those interceptor drones. I need you to stop those incoming missiles. Can you spread the drones out a little and detonate them in their path? They're all locked onto us, so they shouldn't be too hard to intercept. We need to buy Mr. Navarro a few minutes."

"Sounds good to me," said Maxwell. "Will do!"

The three interceptor drones left their positions relative to the Philosopher King and streaked past the point-defense drones to intercept the oncoming missile barrage. Maxwell had them spread apart, and as they closed in on the missiles, they exploded in a bright flash that obscured the outcome for several seconds. Maxwell, along with everyone on the bridge, held his breath until the sensor data cleared. Once it cleared, it became apparent that all but eight of the alien missiles had either been destroyed or thrown helplessly off course. A cheer went up on the bridge. Maxwell prioritized the remaining missiles, and the point defense drones finished them off. Thirty seconds later, the aliens released another barrage.

Spear turned back to Ander. "How long until we can jump?" Spear's voice sounded distorted with the crush of g-forces, and he had to yell to be heard over the near-deafening engine roar that enveloped the bridge. Ander rechecked his calculations. He was targeting a certain interval when the gap would appear. He adjusted the ship's acceleration to arrive inside it the instant it materialized.

"Ninety-two seconds!" Ander called out.

"Not good enough," said Maxwell over the com. "The missiles will catch us about fifteen seconds before we get there, and we have no more interceptor drones."

"Ander, we need another option," said the captain. Ander felt the weight of the universe land squarely on his shoulders. He rechecked his numbers. They were correct, but there was one other option. He could try to make the earlier opening. It was twenty-seven seconds earlier, but it would stay open for four seconds so if he could just shave off twenty-three seconds...

"Hold fast!" Ander shouted as he slammed the acceleration. The twin engines blazed to maximum. Jill Thomas screamed from her console, the captain gasped, and Ander could hear Maxwell grunt over the com as the Philosopher King sprinted with all its might for that one sliver of space, for that one tiny window where it might escape the claws of its pursuers. Ander's vision began to tunnel, and blackness threatened to take him as he moved his fingers as leaden weights across his controls. The ship's drive could bleed off no more of the g-forces that now pummeled them. He could feel the capillaries in his eyes burst as the inertia threatened to crush him and everyone else on the ship.

The missiles came, still gaining. The King's increase in velocity gave scarce breathing room for their target. The window opened, and the wave of gravity pulled back. The seconds stretched subjectively as Ander willed the ship forward to meet it. One second passed, then two. Three seconds were gone as they crossed the final kilometers barely ahead of the alien weapons that had just overwhelmed their point-defense drones. Ander could sense the faltering ebb and the imminent resurgence of the wave of gravity. His hand was already in motion to engage the shadow drive, and, in the final milliseconds of opportunity, the Philosopher King slipped the bonds of solar gravity and became faster than light.

EPILOGUE

Tom Hepner didn't feel so well. First, he'd been zapped by aliens and then some madman up on the bridge tried to crush them all with more gravities than the human body was ever designed to handle. But the human body was resilient, and though he was black and blue and hurt all over, he was still in considerably better shape than his three would-be captors. He was sure two of them were straight-up dead. They looked like deflated balloons leaking some yellow substance that must be what passed for blood in their physiology. The third, still seated in the co-pilot's chair of the mining shuttle, was moving but didn't appear conscious. Earlier, the aliens had seemed to suffer during the mild ride up from the surface. Whatever the Philosopher King did after they'd docked, especially that last bit, was way more than they could handle. He tapped the com.

"Miner one to all teams, what in vacuum just happened?"

"Miner one, this is Miner two. Are you okay? We saw the aliens attack you!" Sara-Jay Schieva's voice came back in answer.

"Yeah, I'm okay," Tom said. "I wasn't sure if anyone noticed that. My guests here have been neutralized. I guess I can thank whatever psychopath was piloting the ship for that."

* * *

The Philosopher King dropped back out of shadow space five light-years out from the solar system in the safety of deep space. Once the ship's gravity well was re-established, Dr. Ellison began triaging those who had suffered the worst from the intense acceleration before the jump. One crew member, twenty-two-year-old culinary specialist Barry Reed, had suffered a fatal aneurysm during the ordeal. The ship's cook was found deceased, strapped into his acceleration chair at the back of the kitchen. There were other serious injuries, including Jill Thomas, who suffered a collapsed lung, but no other deaths. No one on the ship escaped superficial bruising and soreness, except Jax Dyson who had experienced none of the g-forces thanks to the strange technology of the alien craft where he'd remained until they had escaped the system.

* * *

Later that evening, Ander Navarro sat in the mess hall staring down at his meal but not seeing it. His preoccupation prevented him from noticing even when Joshua Spear sat down across from him.

"Hey," the captain said.

Ander looked up startled. "Captain, sir..." he said.

Spear waived his hand as if to swat away the formality.

"How are you holding up?" he asked.

The whites of Ander's eyes, like Spear's, were still blood red, and the two looked like they'd both been in a street brawl. But that wasn't what the captain was asking about.

"I feel guilty," said Ander. "If I hadn't been so eager to activate that space station then..." He trailed off before continuing. "I placed the ship and everyone aboard in grave danger because of my naivete. One of my crewmates died because of it! No, more than that: I directly killed him when I pushed the engines so hard. He died by my own hand on the control lever. Captain, sir, I am so sorry. I'll get my resignation to you by morning, and you can just drop me off at the nearest port."

Spear gave him a sad smile when he'd finished and leaned forward a bit, forcing Ander to give him his undivided attention.

"Listen to me, Ander," he said. "First, I'm not going to accept that resignation. You signed up for two years, and I plan to get at least that out of you, hopefully more. Second, it wasn't your call to activate the space station. That was my call, my responsibility. We were all excited about the prospect of first contact, and if nothing else we did accomplish that! It was my call, and we were all in agreement. We knew there would be risks. I knew there would be risks. This is deep-space exploration. Risk is our chosen way of life. And you didn't kill anyone. The aliens did that. You were busy saving us, and you did that with courage and professionalism. You are exactly the kind of crew member I want on my bridge."

Spear paused and waited for Ander to speak. The younger man looked down at his untouched food for a moment and then back up again.

"Thank you, sir," he said. "I guess the other thing that's bothering me too is that we tried to help the aliens and then they just turned on us. I feel at once naïve for not seeing that coming and also betrayed. When I was in communication with them, they seemed so reasonable and even friendly in an odd sort of way. Should we have left them there? Should we have just ignored them? I guess in hindsight we should have, but that idea bothers me too."

"Well, Ander," Spear said, "the thing you need to realize is that in this broken and imperfect galaxy we find ourselves in, sometimes we can do the right thing ethically, but still suffer for it. There's an ancient idiom that says, 'No good deed goes unpunished.' I don't believe that, certainly not in the eternal sense, but I can appreciate the sentiment of whoever invented it. But our ethics must transcend our circumstances, or what good are they? I guess what I'm trying to say is, I still think that helping the aliens was the right and moral thing to do. Their own immoral actions against us do not negate the good we did, nor would they serve as a justification for us to neglect our conscience."

"Yes, I suppose," Ander acknowledged reluctantly. "But it just turned out so awful."

A little humor touched Spear's eyes as he smiled again.

"That's just life," he said standing up. "Can I count on you again the next time something awful happens?"

Ander looked up at him this time with a small smile of his own.

"Yes sir," he said. "And thanks."

* * *

Joshua Spear, Jill Thomas, Dr. Ellison, and Maxwell Forrester stood around the examination table in the medical bay staring down at the unconscious creature. It was secured to the table with emergency straps, all tentacles and appendages restrained.

"Did it ever regain consciousness?" asked Spear.

"No," replied the doctor. "I know it is still alive because fluids are still circulating inside, though it doesn't have a circulatory system in the sense that we do."

"Is its brain damaged?" asked Maxwell.

"That's a real possibility," said the doctor. "Though I'd be hard-pressed to tell you which of the organs inside functions as a brain. It seems to have a more distributed neural system than most earth life."

"What are we going to do with it?" asked Jill.

Spear considered for a moment. "I think that this is a job for the academic types. We'll set a course for Marcell Colony, they have a good medical university there. Doctor, do you think you can keep it alive until then?"

"I think so," she said. "I've introduced a basic glucose solution based on some compounds I found in the remains of the other two aliens. It seems to be adequate to feed the thing's cells, at least temporarily."

"Good," said Spear. "We'll turn over the alien and the remains of its companions to the university. Hopefully, they'll be able to revive it, but if not, I'm sure they'll be interested in studying its biology."

"Its own people might be able to help it better," said Jill.

"Yes," said Spear. "But their demonstrated ill intentions make returning him to their care impossible. It attacked one of my crew and attempted to board my ship. It'll just have to settle for whatever care human beings are able to give it."

"And what of the ship?" asked Maxwell.

"The ship is another matter," said Spear. "It is ours by right of salvage, but the technology on board will make it a tempting target for powerful interests. That makes us a tempting target too. John has a contact in the navy who he believes can help us and who he swears is trustworthy. We sent a secure message containing an abbreviated version of events and a request that the system be designated as hazardous and off limits to civilian spacecraft. We were very clear about the aggressive nature of the aliens and the potential danger they pose. But we didn't mention the alien ship specifically, merely that we were in possession of an artifact that will require greater security than we can provide. Until we get a response, we will say nothing more about it."

"I agree on both points," said Maxwell. "Given how superior the aliens' technology seems to be, it's probably safer for humanity that they stay bottled up in their system. However, I'm not sure how long we will be able to keep details about the alien craft a secret. Everyone aboard knows about it and that Jax piloted it, though they didn't hear it from him. I didn't have to tell him to stay tight-lipped."

"I know," said Spear. "For now, I'm going to ask the crew to refrain from mentioning it in any long-range communications. I'll try to impress upon them that it's a safety issue. And it really is, especially while our defenses are depleted."

"Do you think the crew will be *able* to keep it a secret?" asked Jill.

"I think most of them understand the potential danger of letting it out of the bag," said Spear. "But I also have Phil monitoring all outgoing long-range communications and scrubbing any references to the craft."

Both Jill and Dr. Ellison seemed a little taken aback, but Maxwell nodded slowly in agreement.

"That'll only work until we reach Marcell Colony," the security chief said.

"I know," said Spear. "But at least that gives John and his engineering team six weeks during transit to take the thing apart and study it in detail. I'd like to know how the aliens manage to compensate for the effects of inertia and acceleration so completely. If we could figure that out, it might mean that I won't find myself writing another letter to a crew member's family the next time we have to leave somewhere in a hurry."

THE END

TECHNICAL ADDENDUM

Shadow Drive: Technical Name: *Hyperdimensional Energy Translation Matrix.* The Shadow Drive works by sending energy into a higher dimension of space-time to push the aspect of the vessel that exists there(its "shadow") to superluminal speeds. This is impossible to do in the three dimensions of normal space as the energy requirement would be infinite. But the aspect of the ship that exists higher up the dimensional scale is less massive, and by compressing energy from three normal dimensions into one hyper dimension, the drive can propel that aspect of the ship far beyond the normal Einstienian limit. Importantly, as a peculiar trick of physics, since the aspect is essentially just another dimension of the vessel, it cannot be separated from its lower three dimensions any more than the length of an object can be separated from its width. Thus, the rest of the ship comes along for the ride. Since the forces propelling the vessel do not exist in normal space, the vessel and its crew don't experience the normal effects of acceleration and inertia that affect all objects moved by normal physical means. In essence, the vessel doesn't move through normal space but rather is teleported along the course, always existing in space-time relative to its hyperdimensional aspect. In a sense, the vessel then becomes *its own* shadow.

Superluminal Pilot Classifications: Superluninal pilots are trained to use a neural interface that translates data about surrounding hyperdimensional space into bioelectrical wave patterns. These patterns convey information about the hyper-dimensional pathways a ship can transverse while its shadow drive is engaged. The ability to interpret these patterns varies from pilot to pilot.

Classification is determined based on demonstrated proficiency, a combination of natural aptitude and technical skill. The Interstellar Navigator's Consortium(INC) was founded in 2421 to establish standards and provide accreditation for pilot training programs. The INC rates pilots on a decimal scale between one and ten based on supervised assessment or transit log data. Ratings are reassessed annually based on ship's data or every five years by assessment.

Generally speaking, a pilot with a higher rating will be able to interpret data from the neural interface more thoroughly and find more efficient pathways for a ship to transverse. This allows the ship to reach destinations more quickly. Because hyperdimensional space is fluid, pathways are always in flux and cannot be permanently mapped over interstellar distances. The pilot must actively read the data in real time and direct the shadow drive manually.

Much research has gone into developing a method to enable synthetic intelligences to pilot a shadow drive. However, all ef-forts to this end have proven unsuccessful with the intelligence unable to properly interpret the information in the way a human pilot does. It is widely believed that this is because, unlike a human mind, they do not exist beyond three-dimensional space.

Type Five Synthetic Intelligence: Synthetic intelligences are classified into five types according to cognitive ability. Type one is the most rudimentary and type five is generally considered the most advanced. When an intelligence emerges inside a neural matrix, it undergoes a series of assessments to evaluate its level of sophistication. A majority of new intelligences receives a rank of type one or two while higher levels appear in only a minority of matrices. However, in recent decades, advancements in quantum engineering have allowed for higher yields of type fives. This has lowered the cost and made them economically feasible for a large range of privately owned spacecraft.